Mind Change

(A Nina Bannister Mystery)

by

T'Gracie and Joe Reese

For information, email **Cozy Cat Press**, cozycatpress@aol.com or visit our website at: www.cozycatpress.com

COZY CAT
P R E S S

ISBN: 978-1-939816-74-0

Printed in the United States of America

Cover by Paula Ellenberger
http://www.paulaellenberger.com/ design

1 2 3 4 5 6 7 8 9 10

To the Adjunct Faculty Members of the Academic
World

*Note: All of the research quoted in this novel comes
from actual academic journals. All of the administrative
offices cited actually exist.*

CHAPTER ONE: A DIFFICULTY IN READING

It was a plain little house and Nina Bannister loved it. It was not, in all honesty, even a house at all. What was it? A bungalow? No. A cottage? That would be putting an optimistic spin on the thing. It was literally no more than an outbuilding, a something that would have passed for slave quarters if slaves had existed at the time of its construction. It contained only one large room, partitioned by half walls and dotted here and there by what passed for a tiny kitchen, a never-quite functional bathroom, a bed nook and, at her first glance, it was semi-coated by badly peeling grey paint seemingly bought as surplus from the German army.

But she still loved it.

Tucked away in this near forest, with a crumbling red-brick wall separating it from the lane, and a delightfully dilapidated off-green swinging gate allowing entrance to the yard-patch—

—tucked away just far enough from the sight of those few university students who might be passing en route to the mile distant campus—

—it looked fine indeed!

It was her Hobbit House and had been for three days now, ever since her Monday arrival on the Ellerton University campus.

These were thoughts that occupied her as she returned to the place, having done a little shopping. She slipped her key into the lock, forced the door open (for it was true that nothing opened, locked, flushed, heated, slid, buzzed, whirred, ticked, cooled, or functioned in any cause and effect manner precisely as it should have in this shadowy, forgotten little efficiency of hers), and walked inside.

Tea.

She crossed the room, extricated herself from the computer-weighted backpack, entered the kitchen, and started the pot boiling.

After a short time the tea was ready.

Music.

A three disc set of *I Vespri Sicilliani*—for lesser-known Verdi was another of her hidden vices—buzzed in furred 1951 tones through the room.

And satisfying herself that Maria Callas was, in fact, singing just loud enough to avoid shrillness and capture genius, she sat before her small table, turned on the black, revolving fan, and opened her computer.

Email.

There it was, glowing white with black messages snaking their way across the screen.

From Margot: "So excited about your new adventure. Have you met your classes yet? Write, write! Tell me everything!"

From Alanna: "Everyone in Bay St. Lucy is excited about your honor. No one deserves it more. The real winners will be, of course, the students."

And a few more, from Macy and Paul (writing from Jackson), and from Tom and Penelope (writing from parenthood), and—

—the usual suspects.

She answered them all, of course.

Then she changed clothes and allowed herself to read a mystery.

Which she had been doing, legs propped on one chair, tea beside her on the nightstand, for sixty or seventy pages. The murder had happened, body discovered, suspects introduced, proper flavor of British countryside added, a few paragraphs of obligatory imagery thrown in, followed by twenty-five pages of dialogue.

She was on, to be perfectly accurate, page 67, when the first event took place to stop her from drifting into pre-sleep: a hard, mid-September rain began to fall, blown in by a breeze strong enough to shake the branches of the oak grove which lowered over her cottage—for it could only be called a cottage when she was reading about England—and releasing several thousand bushels of ripe, ready-to-fall acorns, which exploded like a young war upon the tin roof above her.

Blam Blam Blam Blam Blam!

Anzio Beachhead falls. Corregidor falls.

And still the firing continues.

Blam Blam Blam Blam Blam!

Acorns to the right of us, acorns to the left of us.

And the soft early fall rain intensifying, softening, pattering in the wind, washing the window just above the bed, fluttering the curtains and freshening the Earl Grey scented air around her.

This on page 67;

On page 69, a knock at her door.

Acorns?

Rap, rap, rap.

No, this was a knock. From a human hand.

The acorns were:

BAM BAM BAM BAM

This was:

Rap, rap, rap.

She looked up, putting down the book.

The door's window was curtained, too, and all she could see was a shadowy form moving slowly back and forth, obviously shifting weight from one leg to another.

It had always bothered her that she could only identify someone knocking at her door by opening it.

Which did not seem a particularly secure arrangement.

But this was a university, she told herself, and apart from the occasional disgruntled undergraduate, unhappy with the results of a C+ on what had been a pure B- transcript—apart from this menace, none of the other harsh realities of the actual world existed to threaten its inhabitants.

Still, rising, she found a note of nervousness in her voice as she asked the still wavering shadow beyond the doorway:

"Who is it?"

"This is Rick Barnes. I'm from the local paper. Sorry to bother you so late!"

She got out of bed and made her way toward the door.

The local paper?

What was *that* all about?

She opened the door and saw a tall unkempt figure standing before her. He was dressed in denim jeans and jacket. He had a Kris Kristofferson kind of beard, and, for that matter, Kris Kristofferson blue eyes.

"Ms. Nina Bannister?"

Kris Kristofferson deep voice.

Good that she was a Kris Kristofferson fan.

"Yes, I'm Nina Bannister."

"Once again, I'm sorry to bother you so late in the evening."

"Actually," she said, taking a step back into the living room, "it isn't that late. I was just reading a book and had dozed off. You did me a favor in keeping me from going to sleep. I would have waked up at three in the morning."

"I still have the feeling that I'm disturbing you."

He stepped into the living room, his wild mop of dark gray light gray completely silver blue-black hair explosively disheveled, and somehow giving the impression that it had been combed by an atom smasher.

"Come on in. Will you have a cup of tea? I just made a pot an hour or so ago. You like Earl Gray?"

"Love it."

"Good. Sit down."

He did, somehow folding his long body over a chair and partially under the kitchen table.

She poured and served the tea, savoring it herself as it trickled down her throat.

"You're a newspaperman?"

"I am. Have been for forty years."

"Always here?"

"For the whole time. Ace reporter for *The Gazette*. People ask me why I don't move away, and I hardly know what to tell them. I'm a small town guy, I guess."

"Well, this town isn't that small. It's hardly a mere village. And it has Ellerton University."

"Yes, that's true. And that makes it home."

"You graduated from Ellerton?"

"I did. Degree in journalism, then went straight to work for the paper. So I have ties to the university. And there's always something going on, on campus. Concerts, sports events—I cover them all, as well as the occasional pot bust or fraternity beer brawl."

"The seedier and rougher side of academia."

"Yes. Maybe not the streets of Manhattan, but not completely boring either."

He smiled as he sipped his tea, laugh wrinkles changing their angles and patterns as his expression altered.

"And that," he went on, "is what has brought me here."

"What, exactly?"

"Well, you're big news at the university."

"You're kind to say that. I'm not sure I'm as important as all that. But I must say, I was honored to get President Herndon's letter."

"When did you receive it?"

"A month ago, in mid-August. I still have it, as a matter of fact."

"You do?"

"I do."

"Could I see it?"

"Of course, you could see it. It's over here, in the desk drawer. I'm keeping it safely hidden away, just in case some actual professor approaches me and asks what I, a mere ex-high school teacher and principal, am doing on the campus of one of the state's most prestigious research universities."

She opened a drawer of the desk, took out the carefully typed letter, and laid it open on the kitchen table so they could both read:

Dear Ms. Nina Bannister:

This is President Lucinda Herndon, writing from Ellerton University. I have the honor to inform you that you have been selected as winner of our first Golden Age Teaching Award. You have received this award because you have, for decades, inspired and informed your students, your community—and in short, your world.

We here at Ellerton are proud to recognize you. But we do not wish our acquaintanceship to be that brief, or to consist merely in one speech or one awards event. Rather, we would like to invite you to be a part of our campus intellectual life for the entire fall semester, teaching at least one course in your area of expertise.

You will be given free housing on campus and paid an honorarium of ten thousand dollars.

We hope the funding will be useful to you, but it is we who will be the actual winners. Ellerton wishes to become in reality what many other institutions claim to be, but are actually not. We wish to be a true Teaching University, where every one of our undergraduate students has the opportunity, during each moment of classroom time, to hear and be around a master teacher, a classroom creator whose wit, humor, consideration, love of subject, respect for students—have been honed and developed over a lifetime of work and dedication.

No, Ms. Bannister: we hope you will accept our monetary offer, but it is we who will be receiving the treasure.

Again, it is with deep pleasure that I contact you.

Please—do join us for the Golden Age Semester at Ellerton.

We all look forward to learning from you.

Lucinda Herndon
President
Ellerton University

They both looked at the letter for a time, regarding it as something warm, glowing, golden, and sacred.

"That," said the man sitting beside her, "is quite a letter."

Nina nodded.

"You can imagine how it made me feel."

"No, I really can't. No one's ever offered me a Golden Age Reporter Award."

"Well. Maybe when you get to be my age."

"I'm your age now, and the only thing on my horizon is forced retirement. Anyway, I guess it's time to explain the interruption. I've got a feature coming out in a day or so, and it's going to be about this Golden Age program. And about you."

"I'm honored."

"No, actually we are. Apparently—Lucinda shared this with me—everybody in Bay St. Lucy remembers you as the greatest teacher in the town's history."

"I'm sure that's an exaggeration."

"Not much of one, from what she tells me. And then there's the Lissie movement. That was your idea, wasn't it?"

"It came from a lot of sources. Hopefully it did some good."

"Twenty-three women now serving in Congress who might not have been there without that movement."

Nina shook her head:

"It's a shame. We were shooting for forty."

"Give it time, give it time. But anyway, I know all about those things. Plus some other facts that Lucinda was able to give me. I could pretty much write a decent piece about you as it. One thing though I thought you might clarify."

"If I can."

"Lucinda told me that you two had known each other before."

"Yes. We were at Ole Miss together getting our teachers' certificates. I was already married to Frank, but he had to stay in Bay St. Lucy because of his law practice. Lucinda had not yet met Thomas, the man she was to marry. We were in several classes together and sort of felt like kindred spirits. We became good friends, and have kept in contact. Our lives became quite different, of course. I went back to Bay St. Lucy and the public schools. Lucy met Thomas, whose career became meteoric. President of the great Ellerton University, pride of the state. And then when he died, of course, Lucinda succeeded him."

"Unanimous choice of the board. And a great choice. Lucinda Herndon—everyone will tell you this—is one of the most creative university presidents in the country. If she weren't, then you wouldn't be here. And there are, according to her, going to be many more like you in years to come. Hundreds of great public school teachers, most still in excellent health—living off teacher retirement, probably secretly glad not to do hall duty and eat tater tots anymore."

"Actually I never minded the tater tots."

"But the hall duty?"

"I usually tried to find a football coach to do that for me."

Rick Barnes smiled and shook his head:

"All of that talent being wasted. And most of those teachers never having had the chance to go into a classroom where the students weren't throwing books at each other, and they didn't have to worry about kids getting into fights in the halls. Great teachers, all gathered at a true university. What an idea."

"I don't know. I had to think long and hard about whether I would try to do this."

"What made you hesitate?"

"Well, I have a nice little life in my beach cottage. A nice circle of friends. Bay St. Lucy is comfortable for me, although some rather strange events have happened in the past two years—most of which you shouldn't write about because your readers would never believe them. But Lucy was nice enough to call me personally a few days after the letter arrived. It was good to hear her voice. Somehow the years seemed to melt away. She told me about this little house, and how she could picture me in it for a semester. And the more she told me about my fears, the more she seemed to be able to allay them."

"Those fears being?"

Nina shrugged.

"Just not being, well, qualified to be here."

"Not qualified?"

"I'm a high school teacher. The faculty here are brilliant people. World renowned. I can't teach the things they teach. I can't even understand the books they write."

"And what did Lucinda say to that?"

"She just told me not to worry. That great teaching is great teaching. And that I would always be welcome at Ellerton."

"That," said Barnes, getting to his feet, "is probably the line I'll close the piece with."

Nina followed him to the door.

"I hope it's true."

Another smile back to her:

"It's true. And now I'll let you get back to reading. You need to get some rest. You've got a busy semester in front of you."

"Thank you. I look forward to reading your article, Mr. Barnes."

"I hope you'll enjoy it. And please call me Rick."

"All right, Rick. Take care and have a nice evening."

"I will, Nina. Listen, I've enjoyed getting to know you. I'm sure we'll be seeing each other again."

"I look forward to that."

"Good night then."

"Good night."

She closed the door.

Then she went back to bed and lay down.

She picked up the book and began reading.

She was four pages farther along in the story before she realized that she was thinking of Rick Barnes.

CHAPTER   TWO: PRESIDENT   LUCINDA HERNDON

The campus of Ellerton University was, to Nina's way of thinking, what every campus should be, and looked like all campuses should look. It was a postcard. The president's residence—part of the postcard—was, of course, a two-story, red brick mansion in the turn of the century style, with a circular carport on one side that always would have, she assumed, one or two black limousines parked in it.

And this, she thought to herself as she approached the building—she had walked the half mile from her Hobbit House—was where her old friend Lucy had ultimately found herself.

Was this a dream?

Was she really going to teach at this university for an entire semester?

Was it possible that she was imagining the whole thing, even down to the fact that President Herndon had called her Monday afternoon, just after her arrival on campus, to invite her this Thursday morning to breakfast?

No, the Mississippi autumn air was too perfect, and the scents of the pine trees that dotted campus too fresh.

It was all reality.

And so, squaring her shoulders, she walked onto a kind of veranda, where there were double-glass doors. She rang the bell and waited. The doors were opened by a smartly-dressed young woman who looked as if she would have been a lab assistant of some sort if she hadn't been serving as a greeter.

"Ms. Bannister?"

"Yes, I'm Nina Bannister."

"Please come with me; President Herndon is expecting you."

She was ushered to a wing of the house where a tea service had been set up, and Lucinda Herndon rose to meet her.

"Nina! Dear Nina, it's been so long!"

The woman before her was dressed in a navy blue suit, which set off nicely her short but elegantly groomed shiny-as-a-new dime silver hair. Nina was struck by how youthful she looked. Her skin was radiant in the gray morning light that filtered through a wall of east-wing windows. Makeup subtly but expertly applied, a hint of lipstick, a hint of rouge, and the sum effect was of a woman who is used to leading and knows what she is about.

They embraced, they laughed, they cried, they coffeed, they croissanted, and, of course, they remembered.

For the past, Nina remembered Faulkner writing, is never dead. It's not even past.

And that past stared down at them as they dream/remembered, out of the benevolent-looking eyes of Thomas Herndon, whose painting hung upon the far wall.

And it bubbled up as gas out of the ground as one memory trod upon another and they narrated detailed accounts of sharp memories, inaccurate memories, or just plain lies.

They had both been pretty much the same person at that time in their lives. Small-town Mississippi girls, conservative upbringings, no lurid adventures from youth and none planned or plotted for in the future.

Girls whose greatest sins consisted perhaps in oversleeping and missing class, or misunderstanding an assignment.

They could have been expected to turn out exactly the same.

And yet that had not happened.

Nina had become—actually remained—Nina.

Lucinda had become head of one of the country's leading universities.

What her life must be like, wondered Nina, as the first cup of coffee became the second and the campus surrounding the great house filled with students passing, laughing, flirting, and thinking of everything other than mathematics or literature.

"I love them," Lucinda said finally, exiting from reveries about the past and returning to bucolic reality. "They don't keep me young; nothing can do that. But I continually see myself as one of them. And that helps."

"You look marvelous, Lucy. You really do. Being president agrees with you."

The woman sitting across the table from her smiled:

"I hope I'm doing it well. I'm not Thomas. I haven't his vision. But I did learn from him."

"Do you talk with him?"

"Constantly."

"So do I, with Frank."

"I wish they could be here."

"They are."

"Yes. I suppose that's true. And you are here. I'm so glad of that, Nina."

"Me too. Although I'm a little scared."

"Of what?"

"Oh, it's like I said when you called a few weeks ago. What if the students laugh at me? What if the professors laugh at me? I'm just a high school teacher."

"Don't say 'just.'"

"All right, but you know what I mean."

"No one's going to laugh at you, Nina. But—"

Something happened to Lucinda Herndon's expression at that point.

Nina was not sure how it changed. But change it did.

It darkened, as the woman's eyes seemed to fix on something invisible that was happening beyond the glass wall and out in the middle of campus.

"—but Nina, I have to tell you."

"Tell me what?"

"I'm glad you're here. For other reasons."

"Which are?"

A shake of the head.

"It's difficult to go into now. But I'm going to need you."

"You? Need me?"

"Yes."

"I can't understand why."

"Well, there are several things. You're a prominent leader now, because of your work with the Lissie Party. Everyone admires your accomplishments. I trust you. I trust your judgment when difficult situations arise."

"How difficult can any of this be?"

The darkness of expression intensified, and the gaze toward something unseen grew more focused.

"I don't know. I can't predict the future. There have been some difficulties between me and various faculty members."

"What kind of difficulties?"

"There is always tension between teaching and research. Many faculty members want to have more leave time and less classroom time. The president is often caught in the middle in these matters. But I've reached a decision: if the faculty want less classroom time—very well, that's what they shall get."

"So there's no problem, then."

"There will be a—"

Then she thought for a time, and smiled.

"No. I'll not say more about it now. Suffice to say that there will be a meeting of the general faculty tomorrow morning at nine o'clock. I'd like for you to attend it with me."

"Why, Lucy? I'm not on the real faculty."

"Yes, you are, Nina. More than you know."

"Well, if you want me to. I'd be excited to see some of the professors."

"It will be an exciting meeting, I promise you that. Why don't you come here around 8:30, and we'll walk together to Grierson Hall, where the meeting will take place?"

"Fine."

"What are your plans for the day?"

"Well, I got a call yesterday from the English department. The room they've assigned me for an office is ready. I want to go see it. After that, apparently I'm to be taken over to the administration building. I'm supposed to meet and be congratulated by some of the administrators."

"Wonderful. I'm sure you will enjoy the experience. And it's good that you meet these people today because tomorrow they—"

The president stopped herself.

"—well, never mind that for now. It's just that it may be more difficult to get their full attention tomorrow."

"Because the semester starts next Wednesday?"

"Because of various things that will happen. But, as I say, don't worry about any of them now. Just enjoy the campus. You're going to have an exciting semester, Nina."

"I'm looking forward to it."

"As am I, Nina. As am I."

They both rose, and the young woman who had greeted her showed her to the door.

She walked out into the campus, savoring its smell, its appearance—its very texture.

She did find herself wondering, though, as she made her way toward the red brick building that loomed before her, what was bothering Lucinda.

That dark shadow that seemed to fall over her otherwise bright features.

Well, she decided, probably nothing very serious.

And then she forgot the matter.

Not realizing how completely wrong she was.

CHAPTER THREE: IMPRESSIONS OF ELLERTON

She left and walked to Williams Hall, where the English Department was housed. She was shown to her office, which was bare and somewhat off-putting. She nodded to several people who were typing on computers in rooms up and down the hall, but she found them bare and off-putting too.

Finally, she found herself drawn to a classroom. It looked not too different from any of the countless high school classrooms she had inhabited. Desks, blackboard, overhead projector, window opening out onto the world below, which in this case was the oak-lined campus of Ellerton and not the practice football field of Bay St. Lucy.

She walked in.

And the same thing happened that always happened when she entered an empty classroom. It became a theater. Actors began appearing before her, entire scenes playing themselves out, passions unfolding, and life or death struggles taking place.

She had only to sit in any one of the stark desks and let it all happen.

Beowulf, trapped in the coils of the horrible dragon, unable to move, conscious now that, as the beast breathed fire down upon him, his shield was beginning to melt. The pain as the beast's fangs entered his neck, and the sight of his own blood gushing upward like slender twin fountains. But Wiglaff, good Wiglaff, the only one of his men loyal enough to stay and fight with him—this Wiglaff, somehow slipping a sword into that one hollow and vulnerable spot in the animal's impenetrable scales, lunging, twisting, extinguishing the dragon's fire.

Now a relaxation in the grip of the coils.

And Beowulf, summoning the last of his strength, swinging his own sword blindly, cutting off the dragon's head with the one mighty blow—and dying.

All of this she saw in what others had perceived as an empty classroom.

Could she make the students see it?

Could she build that bridge between the mind of the Anglo-Saxon singer and the minds of the fifteen or so young people who would be sitting here in the next few days?

"Are you new faculty?"

This from a voice behind her.

She turned and saw a slender man of almost indeterminate age, bespectacled, dressed in a gray sweater and blue jeans, and standing framed in the doorway.

"I'm Nigel Davis. I'm a medievalist."

"I'm Nina Bannister. I'm a—Nina Bannister."

"No, I mean, what is your specialization?"

Nina thought about that for a while, gave up trying to think of a specialization, and simply said:

"I'm just a teacher. I was imagining a scene from Beowulf."

Nigel Davis beamed:

"Ah, the seventh century epic! Just a bit earlier than the period I write about. What a peristaltic work though! I remember reading Geddings' thoughts about it last year. I don't know why I would have been reading Geddings. Just playing, I imagine. I do that a lot. But you have to love Geddings, of course. A structuralist, a real Derrida man attacking oral poetry of the early Saxon age. Oh God, what did he write? Well, you can imagine. Something along the lines of: 'the singer (if one can apply that kind of primitive labeling to the rhetor in question) following both kinds of holism which both structuralism and deconstruction seem committed to. Twisting the principal of immanence away from any belief in functioning linguistic states as necessary conditions for intelligible totality.' Don't you just love that stuff?"

Nina paused for a while, and finally said:

"I do. I like it when Beowulf cuts off the dragon's head, too."

But Nigel Davis, the medievalist/structuralist, seemed not to hear, and merely continued:

"It's all so Derrida! Quasi-transcendental as a type of holism. It doesn't even depend on functioning states but rather is just, in itself, a kind of sufficient condition for the very idea of totality. What will you be teaching?"

It took some moments for Nina to realize that she had actually understood the last few words, but she finally did so, and answered:

"Freshman English."

The man before her seemed taken aback:

"They have you teaching freshmen?"

"Yes."

"I thought that was usually done by adjuncts."

"Well, I am a kind of adjunct, actually."

"What do you mean?"

"I'm a high school teacher."

"Oh, I'm sorry. I thought you were in the department."

Nina thought of saying, *I'm a Golden Age Teacher*, but did not know how Derrida might have put that thought, and settled for saying:

"No. I'm not."

"Well. Nice to have met you. All of you people do good work down there. Have a nice time visiting the campus."

With that, Nigel Davis turned and walked away.

Were they all going to be like that? she wondered.

Maybe Lucinda was wrong.

She wasn't anything that ended in *ist*. Not a structuralist, not a medievalist, not a modernist—just a Nina.

Maybe she didn't belong here.

She did not stay *here* for long, there being no laughter in the building and no amity in the hallway—but instead met a young woman who was assigned to be her guide, and was taken by this person to the administration building.

Every university has a suite of offices that are much nicer than anything else on campus, and that seek to imitate life at the highest corporate levels, or what academia imagines the highest corporate levels to be. The floors are carpeted—beige carpeted—the desks wide and expansive, the windows wide and expansive, the music muted and the furniture leather, usually green leather. The president has an office there, as does the Provost or Chancellor, the Vice President, the Bursar—and more people than Nina would have thought possible.

She was led from office to office, and the various university administrators, apprised of her coming were waiting in lobbies to meet her:

The first:

Office of Vice-Provost.

An elderly distinguished-looking man peered at the two of them through the glass wall for an instant or so, standing completely motionless, beside his desk. Then he smiled and beckoned for them to come in.

They did, and he, smiling, ambled toward them:

"Come in, come in. I'm Charles Matheson. I'm the Vice-Provost. It's so good to meet you."

He was a tall, silver-haired, slender man, dressed so impeccably that Nina could not stop looking at his shirt. It was a shirt that had trimming like a tree or a car has trimming. It began as sky blue, but there were fine strips of white running vertically through it, and a collar of the same white, and it was all set off by a superb pair of galluses, navy blue, hooked to his ash-gray slacks by the miniature leather anchors of a pirate frigate.

"So good to have you on campus, Ms. Bannister!"

"So good of you to have me."

"Dr. Herndon—Lucinda—has told all of us about you, and about your exploits. Congratulations on winning the first Golden Age of Teaching award. I'm certain we can all learn from your expertise."

"I'm going to be the one learning."

"Oh, no, no; I can assure you that—"

And from that moment on, the next hour dissolved into a dark murky liquid filled with polite, but essentially meaningless, phrases.

She was introduced to the Assistant Dean of Curriculum Development (*Did he really develop the entire curriculum?* she wondered. *Or did he just assist someone else in developing it? And, she wondered, somewhat morbidly, if he and his direct supervisor were to die suddenly, would there no longer be any curriculum at all?*)

This assistant dean gushed over her for a while, and then he led her to the offices of other administrators.

—all of whom were waiting for her.

The first one led her to the second, and on and on.

"Hi there, I'm Annette Dunwoody; I'm Vice President of Academic Affairs!"

"Nice to meet you!"

"Nice to meet *you!*"

And blah blah blah

And blah blah blah

Then:

"I'm Peter Richards! I'm Director of Associated Degree Programs!"

"Nice to meet you!"

"Nice to meet *you!*"

And blah blah blah

And blah blah blah

Then:

"Hi there; I'm Peter Jarvis. I'm Assistant Vice President for Remediation and Innovation."

"Nice to meet you!"

"Nice to meet *you!*"

And blah blah blah

And blah blah blah

Then:

"I'm Naomi Jannings-Todd. I'm Assistant to the Associate Director of the Business/Public Services Division!"

"Nice to meet you!"

"Nice to meet *you!*"

And blah blah blah

And blah blah blah

Then:

"Hi, there. I'm John Gordon, Associate Vice President of Career and Technical Programs!"

"Nice to meet you!"

"Nice to meet *you!*"

And blah blah blah

And blah blah blah

And more and more of them as the building, an eight-armed octopus, seemed to be digesting her and the aide leading her through it. She could only hope that at some future time, the process of administrative digestion completed, she would be forced out at some inconspicuous nether end.

Procurement Systems Director, Associate Vice President for Research and Planning, Vice President for External Partnerships, Executive Director of Statewide Security and Safety, Assistant Vice President for K-12 Initiatives, Vice President for Business and Computing Technology, and on and on and on and on

As though it would never end!

But it got worse.

There was one more office to visit, one more bureaucrat to speak with.

The Provost.

His was the second largest office in the university, of course (after the president's), and he had the most administrative assistants (three), all of whom smiled at her occasionally as she sat in the waiting room.

The wait lasted fifteen minutes.

Then one of the assistants gestured to her and said, quietly:

"The Provost can see you now, Ms. Bannister."

She rose, crossed the carpeted room, and entered yet another den of administrativeness.

"Ms. Bannister."

A huge man rose to meet her. *He was at least six foot six,* she found herself thinking, *and completely bald.* Head-shaven bald, skin glistening.

He could have been a professional wrestler, and he was made even more evil looking by a sharply pointed black goatee.

"Please, sit down. I'm Charles Iverson, Provost."

"Nina Bannister."

"I know that. It's good to have met you, Nina. I'm sorry you've come."

She paused to let that sink in, then asked:

"Pardon?"

"I'm sorry you've come to teach here. I don't think it's appropriate. I told that to Lucinda Herndon when I found out about her plan. Which was only a week ago."

Nina was shocked.

It was proving to be worse than she could ever imagine.

The professors either ignored her or spoke in a language she could not understand; the bureaucrats bored her silly; and the second highest-ranking academic officer at the university—as well as the biggest man she'd ever seen—opened his conversation by telling her she was not wanted.

What had Lucinda gotten her into?

She had to say something.

So—

"I'm sorry you feel that way."

His voice rumbled.

"I do feel that way. We're a major research university here at Ellerton. Our faculty is populated with top-notch scholars, people at the height of their professions and in the forefront of their fields."

"I recognize that. In fact, a month ago when Lucinda called me and broached the idea of my coming, I said the same thing to her."

"But she didn't listen. She often doesn't listen. That's one of the president's faults. She has many others."

Again, Nina knew little to say.

She was sitting in an elegant, thick-carpeted office, across a mahogany table from a man who'd just told her she was not welcome, and who now was in the process of criticizing her friend from years earlier.

"I don't claim to be a scholar. I—"

"Then you shouldn't be here. You shouldn't go into our classrooms."

"I don't think I can do that much harm."

"You can't do any harm in a public high school. At least, I assume you can't. But we're striving to compete with Harvard, Yale, and Stanford, for research grants, for top-notch scholars and for the best students. Not only in the state but in the country. Now I read this morning in *The Gazette* that we're recruiting retired people from small-town secondary schools."

"Again, I can only say I'm sorry you feel that way."

"I've just gotten off the phone with Mr. Barnes, who wrote the story. I told him in no uncertain terms that he should have checked with me before putting this article into print. Now who knows what news service might get hold of it, and how many people might read it!"

"I suppose he thought that if Lucinda—"

A shake of that massive glistening head and the volcano that was in the middle of the man's esophagus continued its slowly intensifying eruption.

"He didn't think. No one in connection with this project has done much thinking, if any. If the president had to play this little game of hers, she could at least have kept it quiet."

"I assure you, I have kept it quiet."

"But not Mr. Barnes. His story is now out, and within the month it could make its way into *The Chronicle of Higher Education,* making us look like laughingstocks. Do you imagine for one minute, Ms. Bannister, that Stanford University would stock its faculty with high school teachers? *High school?*"

"I don't know what Stanford does."

"Of course you don't. You're not expected to. But I know. Stanford does the same thing Ellerton does. It promotes research."

"And, I would hope, teaching."

The man across the desk from her leaned forward, and she thought she could feel the huge piece of furniture onto which he leaned sink an inch further down into the dark green carpet.

"Teaching is happenstance. It's one of the minor duties of our faculty."

"I've always read that teaching and research go hand in hand."

"Yes, they do. Like sumo wrestlers."

A pause to let these words sink into Nina's mind, much as the desk was sinking into the carpet.

Then:

"The *hand in hand* thing is for our publicity brochures."

"But you don't believe it?"

"No, and no one else at the highest levels of university administration does either. Do you know what I think when I read a *glowing* student evaluation about what a wonderful teacher Dr. Smith or Dr. Jones is? I think 'Fine, there's an effective clown who can make people laugh,' or 'There's a teacher who gives away *A*'s instead of demanding true critical thinking. The good teachers aren't the popular ones, Ms. Bannister."

"So I suppose the mark of a truly great teacher is to be deeply hated."

"The mark of an Ellerton teacher is to be published. And to be published frequently. In the most prestigious journals. Now as far as President Herndon's play-school program is concerned—"

Nina could feel her face blushing, and she could not help whispering:

"I resent your calling it that."

The eyes boring into her narrowed:

"I don't care what you resent. But as far as that program is concerned, its existence makes me even more aware that Lucinda Herndon needs to be replaced. She was a popular choice to succeed a popular president. But she's aging, and her mind is not the mind of a capable administrator."

"You, I suppose, would be the logical one to replace her?"

"In truth, I have replaced her. Most of the latest faculty hires—the important ones—have been my doing. We're hiring more high-level administrators because of my work, and we're hiring more prolific faculty publishers because of my work. As for President Herndon, it's a battle every day to get smaller teaching loads for truly exceptional scholars. And that battle takes up most of my time."

He looked at his watch.

"Now, I'm late as it is, for a conference of college and university administrators I've got to fly to."

"I'm sorry to have kept you."

"I'm sorry too. Sorry for a lot of things. But you needed to know how I feel. And now you do."

"Thank you for clarifying things. I can see myself out."

And she did.

Once outside, she could think of only one thing to say to the young aide standing bravely beside her:

"I need a drink."

A nod.

"Yes, ma'am."

"You're too young to drink, aren't you?"

"Yes, ma'am, I am."

"I'm sorry."

"I'm sorry too."

"Where is the best place to get a drink at two in the afternoon?"

"Nick's, on Franklin Avenue. That's the main street that leads into campus, with all the restaurants and bookstores. Everybody goes there."

"Are all those people we just talked to going to go there?"

"No, ma'am. They're too rich."

"Then I'm going to Nick's."

And she did.

By the time she reached the entrance to Nick's Olde English Tavern (the *e* adding authenticity, of course) a soft early afternoon rain had begun to fall, spattering on the windows of the bookstores and hot dog joints, and making Franklin Avenue a sea of crimson and white (Ellerton's colors) umbrellas.

She entered, wincing a bit and standing in the narrow entranceway to allow her eyes to adjust from early afternoon light to eternal cave-semi-darkness.

The long narrow tunnel that was the town's oldest drinking establishment stretched before her.

Ellerton, in deference to its love of purely scholarly pursuits, had abolished Division One sports a decade earlier, and football, basketball, etc., were played now only at the club level, and supervised by volunteer coaches.

But memories of a storied athletic past remained and covered great areas of the dark mahogany walls now looking down at her. Autographed jerseys, helmets, footballs, baseballs, pictures of one team after another, trophies—this, the walls seemed to be saying, is what a university should be—books and professors be damned!

She made her way along, sliding her palms over the tables, approximately half of which were unoccupied in the early afternoon, but all of which, she assumed, would be filled as day wore into evening

To the right of her were tables, to the left, booths.

White-shirted waiters and waitresses wearing English bowler hats wove their way through the dark, narrow aisles, expertly balancing trays of many greasy substances and pitchers of one frothing substance.

"So, the pet store owner says to the customer, 'This frog can perform oral sex!'"

This from a prim-looking girl who, wearing a formless gray sweater and jeans, was seated at a large table just in front of her.

Somehow she felt drawn to the table and the—how many?—seven, no eight, scruffy academic denizens seated around it.

Was it because she was interested in frogs performing oral sex?

Well, how could one not be?

But it was more than that. It was the wry smiles in the people's eyes.

There were older, younger, men, women, people of indeterminate sexual persuasion, bearded people, clean-shaven people—but they had all been at this table before and they would all be here again. She could tell by looking at them for no more than a second that they all knew both how to tell a story and—more importantly—how to listen to a story.

Three of them—one of each gender—saw her at the same time and said, simultaneously:

"Join us?"

She felt embarrassed.

"I don't want to bother you."

A fourth man, this one mammoth and wild-bearded, rose and gestured to an empty chair, saying:

"You can't bother us, we're adjuncts. Nothing bothers us. But you have to tell us who you are."

"I'm Nina."

The table exploded its response:

"*Hi, Nina!*"

Then the same man continued:

"Want to hear about the frog?"

There was, of course, only one answer to this:

"Yes."

"Then—here! Here's a chair for you."

It was produced, wedged into place around the table, and soon was holding her.

"Hey, can we have another pound glass?"

This to a waiter who replied:

"Sure thing!"

He brought a fruit jar glass with the word *Nick's* stenciled on the side. She took it from him, held it out over the table, and watched as it was filled from one of two pitchers of beer sitting on the table.

She sipped it, then said to the young woman opposite her:

"Tell about the frog."

"Right. Everybody ready?"

Mass response:

"Tell about the frog! Tell about the frog!"

"Ok, so the pet store owner looks at the customer, and then at the frog—who's just sitting there—and he says, 'this frog can perform oral sex.'"

A different woman from the opposite side of the table:

"But do Derrida, the French structuralist!"

"What?"

"Tell it the way Derrida would tell it."

The table again:

"Yes! Derrida and the frog!"

The storyteller nodded and continued:

"Uuuuhhhh—aaaaahhh zo zee customair, he buy zee frog. Two weeks, ahhh plus tard—more late, latair, he return. He say, 'zee frog, he only sit. He do no tang. For two week.' And zee ownair of zee store, he look hard at zee frog and say—'Eeef I have to show you dis *one more time*—"

Eruption of laughter.

Finally, Nina found herself thinking, *I understand something about Derrida.*

The massive man:

"So, Nina, what do you do?"

"I'm teaching here this fall."

Questions now from various people around the table, all of whom seemed to be genuinely interested in her:

"Full time or part time?"

She thought about that for a while and said:

"I'm not really sure what my position would be called."

"Well, you either have to be a part-timer or a full-timer. Because the two groups never meet. Full-timers teach one or two courses a semester and make $80,000 to $140,000 a year. We part-timers teach two courses a semester and get $4,000 tops."

"And, we have no office space!"

"No, no, that's not true! We have the adjunct house!"

"So, Nina," said the woman who'd told of the French non-doing frog, "you're going to be teaching Monday morning?"

"Yes, I guess so. English lit survey."

"What are you teaching?"

"*Beowulf.*"

The young woman beamed:

"God, I love—by the way, I'm Tyra—the scene when he cuts off the dragon's head!"

Nina needed to think for only a second before she said:

"I think I want to be an adjunct."

And thus the issue was decided.

She had another glass of beer, became immersed in story after story, then let herself be accompanied by the entire group to the two-story, ramshackle, adjunct house.

Which she loved.

By late afternoon, her books had been installed in a vacant cubicle.

Tyra had become a friend.

So had many more of them.

None of them were *ists*.

All of them taught two courses a semester and made $2,000 a course.

None of them used words she could not understand.

And she was one of them.

The sidewalks, after a late afternoon shower were glistening in the quiet woods as she made her way across campus and back to her bungalow. She was thinking about how bizarre the academic world around her really was, how different from her archaic halls of ivy perceptions, when an elfin figure of a man slipped up to her and took hold of her arm, just above the elbow. He acted as though the two of them had been long lost acquaintances finally meeting again. He looked up at her with his diamond bright little evil-ferret eyes glittering and said—or rather whispered, his voice hissing through the warm still-moist air—

"Do you want to visit a haunted house?"

She did not know what to say.

He continued to ferret watch, his neck twitching one way, then another, his perfectly triangular, perfectly white-shadow face following each movement of his neck.

She was forced to assume he had a neck because it was invisible, muffled in an impossibly-colored scarf, which, depending on where it was in relation to the blue white buzzing street lamps, was either designed by Jackson Pollack or covered with the remnants of an expensive Greek meal.

"It's not far, you know."

It was as though that statement had decided the matter, because he immediately ceased looking up at her inquisitively and began to gaze straight ahead, his little hands squeezing more tightly on her upper arm, the baseball-sized ball of his red toboggan hat swaying first one way, then the other.

"This is a good time of late afternoon to hear them. And the rain is good. It seems to bring them out. I'm Whittington, by the way. Classics. You're Bannister, the woman of gold. Congratulations on your prize, on your honor."

"Somehow," she said, "I never thought of myself as a woman of gold."

"Then you should begin. It has such a romantic ring to it. But at any rate, congratulations on being golden, for, of course, all superb teachers are golden, even though they are disappearing from our midst. All right; so—here we are!"

It took her a moment to realize they were standing at the back entrance to the library.

He put a hand in his pocket and pulled out a key chain. After searching for a time, he found the one he wanted.

"They gave me a key," he whispered to the door knob, which had just begun to fog over with his breath, when he straightened and, looking triumphantly at her, turned it hard counter-clockwise.

"The last weekend before fall term, the library closes late Thursday afternoon. Apparently, the staff needs Friday, Saturday and Sunday to complete an inventory. Or some such nonsense. Ah. Here we are!"

The metal door opened.

And the darkened library stood before them, all of the desks, tables, shelves, volumes, newspapers, computers, and numberings bathed in an eerie green light.

"Come on! Down here on the ground floor there's nothing. We must go up. We must always go up. In order to hear them."

She followed him into the stairwell.

In the normal world, she might not have gone along with this, of course. She would have gently questioned him, and ultimately led him back to his keeper, or his aged wife, who was probably now wringing her hands wondering where he was.

"Oh, did he do that again?"

"Did he go there again?"

But this was not a normal course of things. This whole day had been so dreamlike, that there was little to deter her from doing a bit more dreaming. And it is, she had always felt, a funny thing with dreams. If one went along with them, simply bought into them, then, after a while, it would be like flying. But if you fought the dream and tried to run away you would fall out of the bed.

So here the two of them were, Whittington needing only a torch to complete the illusion that he was ascending to the battlements of a castle, where some creature had been cornered.

They took the elevator to the eighth floor. He pushed open the door from the stairwell, and they entered the stacks.

Which were deathly quiet, bathed in the same green glow of the first floor, and emitting nothing.

There was not the odor of musty old books.

There was not the odor of anything at all; nor perception of slight movement; nor anything else.

It was just the library, closed.

And now it was silent, motionless, smell-less, sightless (at least of anything worth seeing), tasteless, matterless, energyless, and dead.

Obviously, though, not for Whittington, who began to prowl forward, making his way through the two stacks nearest us, like a hunter through a silent forest.

"Listen," he whispered. "Listen."

And she followed.

Listening.

He stood stock still for an instant.

Then he whispered:

"Audesne haec amphiarae, sub terram abdite?"

She was silent.

He asked:

"Oh, you know Latin, my dear?"

"No. I never had the chance to study it."

Whittington shook his head and said:

"Of course; it's so problematic. It's coming out of this volume; don't you hear it? Don't you hear it being whispered to us? Augustine. But Augustine has it from Cicero's *Tuscan Disputations*, as a reproach to a wavering stoic. And Cicero has it from Aeschylus, who must have written it, according to all we know, in a play that is now lost. Hauntings whispered to hauntings. Ghosts echoing to ghosts."

He shook his head.

"And when I hear it, each time I hear it, I think about all of them, all of them who are gone now. All my old colleagues at the University: Frederick Lattimore. Thomas Herndon. Ariel Polonski. Bunny Davidson. All below the earth now. And do they hear? Do they hear Augustine in their place below the earth? Do they hear Cicero? Or do they hear the clear voice of magnificent Aeschylus himself? Or is it possible that they hear nothing at all?"

He walked on, reaching up first to this volume, then to that volume…

Herodotus.

Lucretius.

Marcus Aurelius.

Virgil.

He took down the volume of Virgil, opened it, laughed:

"Oh this is Magnusson's translation, what a lark! That I should come upon it like this. Tommy Magnusson. We had such times together. I remember him translating the superb lines:

> I seemed to see Hector, most sorrowful, black
> with bloody dust, torn, as he had been, by
> Achilles' car, the thong-marks on his swollen
> foot—

He looked at Nina as though expecting a verdict:

"Well, it's not bad, is it? I would have questioned *car*, save for the meter. Oh, Tommy! You did not render it badly, Tommy, nor could you have, for you loved it so much."

He moved on down the narrow space between stacks of books, tapping this one gently on the spine, or chastising that one for looking dusty, or being torn about the cover.

Finally, without looking back at Nina, he said:

"There's a table over there by the window. Let's go and sit down a bit. We can still hear them whispering. But I must admit, I'm a bit tired."

She followed him to the table, which sat next to a large window. She could see a few lights in the buildings, but the campus was obscured by tree limbs.

Despite that fact, he waved toward the window, indicating in the general direction of the bell tower.

"Down there, on the west side of Reed, there used to be something of a faculty club. I remember having cognac there. Of course, there were several places around town where we did that. Gibbons' Pub. That was Ariel's favorite. Ariel Polonski. A magnificent Shakespeare scholar. Shakespeare's plays, all of them, were constantly playing in that mind of hers, apparently simultaneously. After a glass of something or other, she could be prevailed upon to perform. It would be very quiet in that corner of Gibbons—and where Ariel sat, that chair, would become the stage. And the terrible, murderous, insane, deceived Othello would enter. 'Put out the light, and then put out the light.' 'But once put out thy light, thou cunningist pattern of excelling nature, I know not where is that Promethean heat, that can thy light relume.' And then of course, later in the act, Emilia, brave Emilia, discovering the monstrous evil of her husband, Iago: looking at him whispering to him: 'You told a lie; an odious, damned lie; a wicked lie. She false with Cassio? Oh, villainy, villainy, villainy!'"

He shook his head, slowly.

"How you did love the students, Ariel! Dear Othellian Ariel. And far below, *sub teram abite*, in your dark subterranean home, your home below the earth. Lucy is a magnificent president, isn't she? She was Lucy then, of course. Tom and Lucy Herndon. You know, we were a faculty then. And then we watched, over the years, as it all began to slip away. Just dissolve. It became so chillingly competitive. Until the point—"

He looked quickly upward, as though catching sight of Thomas Herndon's ghost floating by, moving from one volume to another:

"Something's going to happen tomorrow," he whispered.

"Pardon?"

"Tomorrow. It will happen tomorrow."

"What will?"

"I was having a glass of brandy with Lucinda last week. We don't do that often these days. I've become too old, and drink disagrees with me. But she had invited me to the residence. I remember her looking at me so strangely and saying, 'What I'm going to say to them, Arthur—well, I shall say it to you, too. But it isn't meant for you, not really. You're different from the rest of them. You should know that."

Nina leaned forward and said:

"She told me she was going to give in to the faculty, and let them have more time to do research."

"So that is what she told you."

"Yes."

"Well. That is in fact the rumor. All over campus."

"So all the professors should be happy."

He merely shook his head:

"All the professors cannot be happy. Not anymore. Not the real professors, anyway."

"Why not?"

"Because, my dear, all the real professors are dead."

And, so saying, he rose and tottered away.

CHAPTER FOUR: A MESSAGE TO THE FACULTY

Nina arrived at the president's house at eight thirty, to find an entirely different atmosphere than the one she remembered from the previous day.

Everything was business. Lucinda Herndon greeted her warmly, of course, but seemed preoccupied with a thousand other matters that needed to be attended to.

She did find time to talk to the young woman who was her personal aide:

"I assume the letters went out, Megan?"

"Yes, ma'am. Every one of them. Morning post."

"Good work. Now, you have a class, I think?"

"Yes. Math at nine thirty."

"Well. Good luck with it. I'll see you tomorrow, then."

"Have a good day, Madame President."

"Oh, I shall. And now, Nina, let us go and meet the faculty!"

She threw open the veranda doors, smiling back at Nina and saying:

"I feel so—so *dramatic* when I do that! And then the walk across the veranda, and past the rose bushes—and out onto the campus! Come! Come, let us begin our day!"

And they walked into the campus, bending into a slight and invigorating north breeze and avoiding Frisbees.

"Dear young Megan is my salvation. The university pays her such a pittance to work for me part time. She's a secretary, greeter, organizer. I don't know what I

would do without her. We had an immense mailing that
went out this morning. She had to supervise it. These
things, although they might seem to, do not get done by
accident."

"No. I'm sure they don't."

"Good morning, Madame President!"

"Good morning, Linda. Good morning, Susan."

Lucinda Herndon smiled:

"It's such an archaic title. 'Madame President.' I
shouldn't allow the use of it. Doctor or Mrs. Herndon
would be fine, and, I suppose, more appropriate. But
the undergraduates have always insisted on it."

On they walked.

Meyers Hall.

"Good morning, Madame President."

"Good morning, Stephen."

She seemed to know each one of all fifteen thousand
or so students on campus.

What had Nina read about Ellerton?

Over a thousand full-time faculty and more than a
hundred upper-level administrators.

She probably knew every one of their names, too.

Grierson Hall was directly in front of them now, and
they could see a larger than normal mix of faculty
members shuffling up the concrete stairs.

"You're looking good this morning, Professor
Herndon."

"Thank you, Professor Clarendon. How is the
anthropology department?"

"Clicking along. A bit concerned about the latest
news on sabbaticals."

"I know. Isn't it depressing? But we'll deal with it
this morning."

"I'm sure we will."

They threaded their way into the main Grierson
lecture hall to find that Rick Barnes had already arrived.

"President Herndon!"

"Hello, Mr. Barnes!"

"And Nina Bannister, the prize winning teacher!"

"Hello Rick," said Nina, taking the hand that was offered to her. "That was a great story in this morning's paper."

"I'm glad you liked it, but it doesn't do you justice. So, President Herndon, I assume you'll be introducing Ms. Bannister to the faculty this morning? I also assume you know the rumor?"

"And what rumor is that, Mr. Barnes?"

"That you've somehow found a way to bend the law."

"That law being?"

"The one that keeps adjuncts from teaching more than two courses a semester. As it stands, if they do, you have to pay them benefits. But if you could get around that law, then you could double the number of courses adjuncts teach—without having to hire more adjuncts, there not being enough room for the ones now working here—and you could drastically cut the faculty teaching load. Which is what they've always wanted, of course."

"Well, there is some truth to that rumor. I think I can tell you that I have, in fact, found a way to clear much more time for the faculty to do research."

"Then they'll love you."

"We'll see. We'll see."

It took a few minutes for the faculty to filter in. During the time, Nina tried to avoid thinking of her own days as an undergraduate.

They had not been spent at this university, but she decided all universities were pretty much the same in certain respects. There was always a big lecture hall. It had the same smell, the smell of *nervous*. There was always a huge green blackboard, always a screen to be pulled down for PowerPoint or whatever kind of presentations were to be given; always the soft laughter turned to soft whispering turned to near silence turned to silence as the professor fixed his microphone, arranged his notes, and began.

This time the professor was not Nina's old chemistry teacher (God how she'd hated chemistry!) but a large, beefy, white-bearded professor whom she'd seen some minutes before, arriving in a big game hunter's hat, not quite a cowboy hat, but a hat with what seemed like animals' teeth stuck in its band, as though he were on not a Midwestern campus, but a Western African antelope plain.

"I want to thank you all for coming. We have a bit of business today. As you know, President Herndon has agreed to join us, to talk about freeing time for more research."

Lucinda stood, turned, and was welcomed by a few pleasantries, a smattering of applause.

"I think the president knows we have some concerns."

More laughter, somewhat nervous this time.

"But I want to point out that we are always happy to have her among us, and I'm sure she'll do her best to answer our questions. So I give you President Herndon."

She walked up the two stairs to the stage, crossed to the podium, leaned forward, resting her forearms on it for just an instant, then seemed to rock back again. She looked around the room, appraising her audience.

How many people? Nina wondered.

Three hundred or so?

The rest not yet back, for classes were still days away from starting.

Then Lucinda Herndon said:

"You are all fired."

She left the podium, descended the three steps leading down the stage, walked to where Nina and Rick Barnes were seated, looked down at them, and said:

"Let's go."

They rose. As Nina followed from the hall, she heard some raucous laughter and a few comments such as:

"That's what we were going to do to you!"

From two or three of the people in the back of the hall:

"Inappropriate humor. Entirely inappropriate."

Then silence, or, at least, sounds that Nina could not hear.

Within a minute, the three of them were outside.

Of all the things that Nina could remember about that morning, that afternoon, the following night—all of it—the walk away from Grierson Hall was the most vivid. She could remember marveling at how still everything was. A few hooded Frisbee players were still running about on the green, but other than those few shrill sounds, and chiming from the Bell Tower across campus, there was simply silence.

Broken by Rick Barnes, who asked:

"My God, Dr. Herndon—what happened?"

"I fired the faculty. Also a great portion of the administration. All in all, I believe 1,263 letters went out this morning."

"But—I mean—is it a joke or a demonstration or—"

"No."

And they kept walking.

There were only two things possible, Nina could remember thinking: either Lucinda Herndon, her old friend, had lost her mind or she was beginning to lose her mind. Despite the radiant glow that she seemed to exude, even as they walked through the brisk morning air, her cheeks flushed a healthy red—despite those things, she had to be suffering from early stages of dementia.

Or she would not have done what Nina had just witnessed.

Barnes again, stammering now:

"I mean—can you do that? Just—fire everyone?"

"Yes."

"But why are they fired?"

"Because we can't afford them."

"But they're the teachers!"

"No they're not. Adjuncts are the teachers."

"But the faculty—"

"They're nothing. And I'm tired of supporting them. Now—I believe we are to part for now. I would suggest that you return to the offices of your paper, downtown. Nina, I think you should go with him. I'm not going to be good company for a time now. You're the person I trust most to counsel me in the days ahead. Also, there's a huge job I'm going to be tasking you with, and quite soon. I'm lucky to have you on my side, and I want you to remain closely apprised of what's going to happen. A good many of the letters will have been received by now, and there will be much activity in the next few hours. Much of it will be filtered through the newspaper office."

"But, Lucinda," said Nina, "I'm not sure how I can help."

"I'll let you know that early this afternoon."

"But whatever's happening is so completely out of my league—"

A shake of Lucinda Herndon's head:

"No it isn't. You seem to thrive in difficult situations. This one is going to become very difficult. I need you, Nina. I apologize in advance for involving you."

"Don't worry about it, if I can really help."

"If anyone can, you can. That's all I can say for now. Please take her with you, Rick. Keep her in the know. And take her advice."

"All right, I will, but—Dr. Herndon, do you really want me to write this story?"

"Yes. That's why you were invited to the meeting."

"I mean—really, you've *fired* them? *All* of them?"

"That's correct. Here—"

She handed him a small, sealed, manila folder.

"The letters are in there. There are two of them—one for faculty, one for administrators. You may quote the letters for your story; or you may reproduce them in their entirety. It's up to you."

"Every faculty member got one of these?"

"Every full-time faculty member will receive a copy today."

"But they're prestigious scholars!"

"Not one university will offer one of them a job. Not one. Not Harvard. Not Oxford. Not even the local community college. That's how prestigious they are. No, dear. They aren't prestigious at all. They're simply arrogant."

"And your reason for firing them?"

"Is that they are crooks."

"You want me to write that? Your quotation is, "The entire full-time faculty is crooks?"

"That's right. They take a great deal of money, and they give nothing back, except specious *research*, which consists of innumerable books and articles that deal with nothing that is taught here on the campus, or anywhere else. They have run, for decades now, a colossal scam. A colossal fraud on the people of a state desperate to avoid going broke. And I'm tired of it."

"But doesn't the Board have to agree?"

"The Board will meet later this morning. They have a regularly scheduled, monthly meeting at ten o'clock.

If they choose to fire me and go on being robbed, so be it. But I will have some things to say to them before that happens. And by the way, I'd like for both of you to be there."

"I—my editor probably has to—"

"I'll call your editor. He'll agree. This story is yours now. If you want it, of course."

"Of course I do."

"Then good. Run along now, both of you. I shall be in touch."

And she left.

The office of *The Gazette* was in chaos. Nina had never seen such confusion. Reporters were running from table to table, cubicle to cubicle, going toward one wall and then changing direction and going back toward the other wall. All the phones were ringing. No one was sitting down, at least not for long. From the street came the sound of sirens. She had no idea whether they were responding to the normal morning fender bender just like those that might have taken place in little Bay St. Lucy, or the riot that she assumed was about to begin on campus.

Two people—white-shirted and disheveled—stared at Barnes and asked, simultaneously:

"Have you heard?"

"Yes."

"Can you believe this?"

"I can believe anything."

"Rick?"

"Yes, sir. Nina, this is my editor, Penn Robinson Jr. Sir, this is Ms. Nina Bannister."

"Yeah, the subject of your story this morning. Good morning, Ms. Bannister."

"Mr. Robinson."

"Do you know anything about this?"

The editor was a compact man with a hatchet face and an intense stare, fuzz-headed and immensely powerful-looking through the chest. He could not have been more than five feet seven inches tall, but intense, beady eyes and massive biceps made him a frightening figure.

He walked toward both of them, a cup of coffee in his hand, steam rising from either the coffee or from him.

"I don't know," she said, "any more than you do."

Barnes:

"Sir, we've just come from Herndon. Apparently she and Nina are very close. She asked me if I'd help keep Nina apprised of everything that's going on. I hope you don't mind her staying close with me on this."

"I'll be happy to have her around. Hell, I'll put her on the payroll if she can help us make sense of this lunacy! Now come on in here, both of you."

He whirled and charged toward a glassed-in partition that obviously served as his office.

When the three of them were seated, he asked Barnes:

"What the hell is going on?"

"She fired everybody."

"This is not a joke?"

"It's not a joke. Here—"

Barnes produced the manila envelope.

"—here are the letters."

He then ripped one of them open and read aloud:

Dear Sir/Madam:

The university wishes to thank you for your services rendered in the past. We will not be needing you after today. Good luck in future endeavors.

Sincerely,

Lucinda Herndon

There was, for a time, silence.

There had to be, she remembered thinking, silence.

Who could say anything to that?

Finally, Penn Robinson sat on his haunches, so that his face was a little lower than Nina's. He put his palms on her knees. With exaggerated calmness as though he were trying to verify that the D-Day Invasion had, in fact, begun, he asked:

"She fired how many people?"

"Twelve hundred and sixty three."

"Oh, my God. Has she lost her mind?"

"I don't know."

"Why were you even at this meeting, Rick?"

"She called me a couple of days ago and asked me to attend."

"Why didn't you tell anybody?"

"I didn't think anybody would be interested. I just thought she was making some announcement about adjuncts getting more courses to teach, so the full-timers would have more time for research."

"She gave you no idea this was happening?"

"None."

The sound of sirens intensified.

Everywhere office telephones were ringing. Or rather landline telephones were ringing. The other things that served as phones—cellphones, iPods, whatever—were making the signals they used to get attention—buzzing, growling, playing Sousa marches. It all sounded to Nina like a circus midway except with more urgency.

"So—what actually happened this morning?"

"We all walked together to Grierson Hall—the president, Nina, and I," said Barnes. "She got up in front of the faculty, told them they were all fired, and left."

"What did they do?" asked the editor.

"Nothing."

"Nothing?"

"Well—they were kind of stunned, I guess. She didn't really give them much time."

"So—I mean—did she tell you why she fired all these people?"

"She said they were all crooks."

"She actually said that?"

"Yes."

Robinson scrunched closer to Barnes, increased the pressure of his fingers around his knees, and ratcheted up the intensity of his gaze. "This is very important, Rick—"

"Yes?"

"Has she lost her mind?"

He shrugged:

"She seemed—seems—perfectly normal to me."

"Ms. Bannister, you're close to her?"

Nina shook her head:

"I'm sorry to say I'm not really that close. We got our teachers' certificates together years ago. We've kept in touch. But our lives were very different. I've spent most of my life as a high school teacher."

"I know, I read Rick's article. Congratulations on the prize."

"Well, it doesn't seem very important now."

"Ms. Bannister, have you had much contact with Lucinda Herndon—well, recently?"

"She called me several times in the last month to ask me if I would come to Ellerton and teach for a semester."

"And she seemed normal?"

"Perfectly. Also, we had breakfast yesterday morning. Nothing the matter as far as I could tell. We just reminisced about old times."

"Old times."

"That's all."

"She's not raving about her dead husband, or claiming that the governor needs to be institutionalized? She's not wearing underwear outside her clothes?"

"No," interjected Barnes. "She's just calm, chipper––boss, she seems normal."

"She just accused—for print—1263 people of being criminals—and you think that's normal?"

Rick Barnes shook his head:

"I didn't say firing a faculty and staff was normal; I just said *she* seemed normal. If she has Alzheimer's or if she's just gone nuts, I can't tell it from her behavior, except, of course, that she's just done something completely insane."

"I'll say it's insane."

The door to the cubicle exploded open, and a young dark-haired woman entered.

"Mr. Robinson, the Associated Press is on line three."

The editor stood bolt upright and then looked down at Barnes:

"Write this story. Write it quick, and then bring it to me. The AP will have it all over the country in ten minutes."

"Yes, sir."

"And don't write anything about the faculty being crooks."

"That's what she said."

"No, she didn't. Not for our newspaper, anyway."

He left.

"Come with me, Nina, over to my little space. I'm going to write this as fast as I can. You're an English teacher. Proofread it after I finish."

In a little more than two minutes, he handed Nina a sheet of paper, on which was written:

Dr. Lucinda Herndon on Thursday morning at nine a.m. announced the dismissal of 1263 faculty and administrators. She made the announcement at the faculty's called monthly meeting. All affected personnel also received news of their dismissal by mail in letters sent the same morning. The president had no comment concerning the university—nor, at the time of this writing—

He got up, walked out of the cubicle and shouted:

"Has anybody gotten hold of anybody else at the university?"

No answer.

nor, at the time of this writing, had university spokespeople

He looked at Nina and asked:

"Is that all right?"

"No," she answered. "It's the most insane article I've ever read."

"I didn't ask if it was sane. Is it grammatical?"

She nodded and said:

"It's as grammatically correct as anything can be that doesn't make any sense at all."

"Okay then."

They walked together across the room:

"That all right, boss?"

"Yeah, yeah, it's fine. Somebody get this out to the AP. Now, we've got to have a comment from the university. Who's next in line to the president?"

Answers kept coming from the ring of reporters, who responded like a popcorn chain in hot oil:

"The Provost."

"Somebody call him?"

"I did."

"What's the story?"

"The Provost is at a conference in Hattiesburg."

"What about the Vice Provost?"

"Taking the day off."

"Well, who's—dammit, who's next in line?"

"Boss—"

"Yes, talk to me, somebody!"

"I've got the Associate Vice President for Curriculum Development on line five."

"What does he have to say?"

"She."

"Okay, what does she have to say?"

"She doesn't know anything about it. Says she'll check into it."

"Where is she?"

"She's at a breakfast, over in the capital."

"Isn't there anybody on campus?"

Pop pop pop reporter popcorn balls.

"Where," Penn Robinson bellowed, "is everybody? What about Public Relations?"

"I've just talked to them."

"And?"

"No comment."

"Damn! Damn!"

"I've got something here!"

"Okay, give!"

"I have the Assistant Dean of Continuing Education on the line."

"Will he give us a quote?"

"Sir, will you be willing to give us a quote?"

Pause.

Shake of the head.

"He's trying to set up a meeting, but no one seems to be on campus."

"Why is no one on campus?"

"It's Friday."

"Okay, that's it. Everybody go sit down."

"Boss, I—"

"But, sir, we—"

"Mr. Robinson, I think—"

"Just go sit down, dammit!"

Nina, and everyone else, did as they were told.

"Now turn off your cellphones. Take the receivers of the other phones off the hook."

She found it strange. A hush fell over the newsroom. There was no clattering from computer keyboards, no growling of little blue plastic boxes, no shouting or murmuring or whispering or laughing or crying—there was no anything that made a newspaper what she'd come to believe that it was, or should have sounded like.

She was simply aware of an awesome feeling that something important had happened, or was happening, and none of them knew what it was or what to do about it.

"Mr. Barnes?"

"Yo."

"Where is the president now?"

"As far as I know she's in the residence."

"Is anybody with her?"

"I don't know."

"Get over there. Ms. Bannister, I think it would be good if you would go, too. If anybody ever needed a friend right now, it's got to be Lucinda Herndon."

Nina sat forward and said:

"Of course, I'll go. But Mr. Robinson—I don't know what to say to her."

"Who does?"

"I have to know: do you think Lucinda is in danger?"

A shrug.

"She's not the most popular woman in the world right now, I can tell you that."

"I'm trying to make sense out of all this. I don't think Lucinda has gone crazy. Maybe this is just a way of making a point."

"What point?"

"Perhaps it's a kind of joke. She's had tensions with the full time faculty. This could be her way of saying, 'All right, if you want time to do research—well, I'll give you *all* your time to do research."

"You actually think this is what she's doing?"

"I'm just trying to interpret events the way Jane Austen might."

"Jane who?"

"It doesn't matter. But I do want to go to her. Maybe if I can talk to her, we can clarify this before anything awful happens."

"Okay, Rick. I'm thinking it might be easier for you to get a real interview with the woman if you've got Nina with you. But if you can get to her, and talk sense with her, you better do it now. Before somebody goes over there with a machine gun."

"Okay, we're gone."

They left the newspaper office, and within five minutes were walking across a campus that, at least for the moment, looked perfectly normal.

Barnes' cell phone rang.

"Yes, boss?"

Nina could hear the tinny rasp of voice coming through the speaker:

"What does the campus look like?"

"Just—the campus."

"Nothing happening?"

"Nothing. Deserted as a tomb. A few people walking here and there. What have you guys been able to find out?"

"Okay, the faculty is meeting in emergency session in Grierson Hall. That's the meeting you were in."

"You want me to go by there?"

"I've sent Sanderson; you just get to the president's house and find out if she'll see you. See if you can get a longer statement. Ask her if she's lost her mind."

"Really?"

"No. But we damned sure better ask somebody."

"Have you found any administrators?"

"No. All we're getting are answering machines. Even the damned secretaries are out of town."

"Well, it's—"

"I know, it's Friday."

"You can't talk to anybody?"

"The Assistant Vice Director For Technical Services."

"Does he know anything?"

"Just that the computers are down. He promises to have them running within the hour. Now see if you can get to Herndon. We're holding the wire open for you."

They made their way through what seemed a small commons between McVickers and Reedy Halls, spied Grierson Hall through an opening of the oak trees, and resisted an urge to go and listen in on the faculty, who by now would be screaming. Here and there, she saw a police car prowling the streets, but nothing seemed urgent.

Nina remembered thinking to herself that this couldn't be happening and wondering what the next step would be.

Some time, before all of this was over, a doctor would have to be consulted. Surely, something very terrible was happening to the mind of her friend Lucinda Herndon.

But what was she going to do about it?

Why was she, of all people, in the middle of this thing?

There was a small cupola in the middle of the major quadrangle, and they had just reached it—the residence itself stood four hundred yards further, beyond the softball and soccer field—when a group of five undergraduates approached them, with the same eager wide-eyed look of people who might be selling raffle tickets.

One ultimately reaches that point in life where all young people look the same. Nina had passed that point some years ago, and so the only difference she was able to detect was basic gender—which on modern campuses these days is not as easy as it might have been in other times—and color of sweaters. The colors of these sweaters—as well as hoods, parkas, backpacks, snow pants, and boots—were red, red, yellow, golden brown, red, green, and yellow again.

One of them spoke to Barnes:

"Sir—"

Yellow pants.

"Sir, do you work for the newspaper?"

"Yes, I do. I'm Rick Barnes."

"Did they just fire the faculty?"

"Yes."

"Are you kidding us?"

"No."

"The whole faculty?"

"Yes."

"Why?"

"I don't know."

"Who fired them?"

"The president."

"President Herndon?"

"Yes."

"When?"

"This morning."

"Oh, my God! Are we still going to have classes?"

"I don't know."

"Can we just, like, go home?"

"I don't know that either."

"This is so cool. This is—are you sure about this?"

"I was there."

"Party! Party party party party *party*!"

And—

"They fired the faculty! They fired the faculty! They fired the faculty!"

And—

"Thank you for telling us!"

"You're welcome."

And off they trundled.

Barnes' cell phone rang again.

"Yes?"

"Mr. Barnes, this is Lucinda Herndon."

"Yes, President Herndon. Nina and I were walking to the residence. We thought we might talk with you."

"No, not at this time. I see that your story is being circulated by the Associated Press."

"Yes, ma'am."

"I've had a chance to read it. Nicely done."

"Thank you."

"It was brief but to the point."

"Well, I didn't want to be inexact, and I wasn't sure about a good many things."

"Of course not. But that will change. I just wanted to remind you: The University's Board of Regents is meeting this morning at ten o'clock in the Executive Office of the Student Union Building. I want you to attend. Along with Nina."

"Are the two of us allowed to sit in Board meetings?"

"No. Try to be there a bit early, will you?"

"All right."

"Good. I'll see you then."

"All right. See you at ten o'clock."

"I'll look forward to it."

And she hung up.

Nina:

"She wants us to go to a board meeting?"

"Apparently."

"How can I do that, Rick?"

"How can you not?"

He dialed a number.

"Boss?"

"What is it? Have you talked to the president?"

"Yes."

"Are you with her now?"

"No."

"Why the hell not?"

"She won't see us."

"Why the hell not?"

"Don't know."

"You're *supposed* to know, aren't you? What do we pay you for?"

"Board meeting."

"What?"

"You pay me to go—along with Ms. Bannister, whom you do not pay—to the Regents' Board meeting at ten o'clock in the Executive Suite which, by university code, we're not allowed to attend, but which she wants us to attend and I think she'll get her way. You don't pay me much, but that's what it's for."

"She invited you to that?"

"Yes she did."

"Go."

"Thought I would. You want us to come back to the office now?"

Pause.

"No. No, goddammit, do something useful, but stay away from here!"

"What's happening?"

"Chaos is happening. Wives, mothers, other newspapermen—people are running around here like chickens with their heads cut off. The only problem is, everybody's asking us questions and nobody's telling us anything! We've had something like twenty calls from parents wanting to know if there's still a university, and what happens to their tuition money."

"Those are good questions."

"Go find me some answers. I don't care how you do it; be a reporter!"

Barnes put the cell phone in his pocket.

"So what do we do," Nina asked, "between now and the board meeting?"

He thought for a time, then pursed his lips and said, quietly:

"Let's go to my place and get a cup of coffee. Then let's go see Adam Marsh."

"Who's Adam Marsh, Rick?"

"He's a lawyer in town, and an old hunting buddy of mine. We shoot doves together. He has an office just off Main Street. Come on. Like I say, we'll have coffee at my place for fifteen minutes or so. Then we'll see what we can find out from Adam. Maybe a lawyer can tell us whether she really has the power to fire these people, or whether they can sue her. Or whatever else he might know."

They began walking.

And the same disturbing feelings began to rise in Nina.

It was easy being with this man.

Too easy.

It remained too easy as they approached his two-story frame house which, as he explained, was the one he grew up in.

It remained too easy as she threw herself on his battered couch and let her shoes fall onto his shag carpet.

It remained too easy as she sipped coffee and, thinking of the fate of her friend Lucinda, asked him:

"Rick, what's going to happen at this board meeting?"

He shrugged.

"There's only one thing that *can* happen. Once they find out what Herndon has done, they'll have to fire her. Immediately."

"But what will they do after that? Apologize to the faculty? And the administration?"

"I don't know, Nina."

"And are the faculty actually fired? I mean, just because Lucinda told them they were?"

"I don't know that, either. Just like I don't know what the board is going to say to the three thousand or so newspapers around the country that are just now getting, and running, the story. I don't know what the faculty is doing in this emergency meeting that they're supposed to be having now. I don't know what the students are doing, other than celebrating."

"There's one good thing about this, Rick."

"What?"

"It's your story. You're now famous."

"Yes. The most insane cock and bull story to come over the wires since—well, since what? What in all of history has happened that's anywhere as unutterably stupid as this?"

"World War II?"

"That made perfect sense, compared to this. And it didn't affect nearly so many people. Okay, so a few Frenchmen got upset when Hitler marched into Paris. But that's nothing compared to what the entire faculty and staff must be feeling now. No, it's all just stupid. And I get credit for writing it."

"Still, maybe you'll win a Pulitzer Prize."

"If I don't get locked up first. If Lucinda doesn't get locked up."

"That's not really funny, you know."

"I know, Nina. I know. But, come on, we've got to time this right. We just have time now to get some info from Adam, then get over to the board meeting."

She put the coffee cup away and slipped her shoes back on.

Why is this man so easy to talk to? she asked herself.

It was the chain of crazy events that were whirling around them.

Anybody would be easy to talk to, given all these insane goings on.

That's why he's so easy to talk to.

She followed Rick to the door of the house.

Somehow though, she knew she would be back.

Adam Marsh's law office was a fifteen-minute walk, and Nina, legs much shorter than the man she was trying to keep up with, was out of breath when the two of them arrived.

They sat in a crowded waiting room for a short time, but then the door opened and Adam Marsh came out to meet them.

"Rick, come in. Haven't seen you in a while."

"Hey Adam! This is Nina Bannister.

"Nice to meet you, Ms. Bannister!"

"Same here."

"Sit down, both of you."

They did.

Marsh's full beard was completely white, but he was still an athletic-looking man, although he walked with a pronounced limp

"Sorry I can't give you much time. It's chaos in here. As I guess you understand. Now come on and tell me: what the hell is going on at the university?"

"I don't know."

"But you wrote the story!"

"You think that means I know something?"

"We've had fifteen calls from faculty and staff in the last hour asking if they can sue somebody."

"Can they?"

"Sure. You can sue anybody."

"Can they win?"

"That depends. It might help me to know *what the sam hill is going on!*"

"The president fired the faculty."

"The whole faculty?"

"Yep."

"Just like that?"

"Just like that."

"Oh, my God."

"Lot of people are saying that."

"Who else did she fire?"

"Administration."

"How many?"

"All."

"What?"

"All."

"Every administrator? She fired every administrator?"

"Yes, she did. I heard her do it; I read the letters."

"I'll be goddamned! How many people is that?"

"Twelve hundred and sixty three."

"I'm going to need a drink."

"Better get one quick. The liquor stores will be running out."

"So—how are you two involved in all this?"

"Nina's a good friend of hers and smart as a whip. On the other hand, I barely know her and I'm dumb as dirt. So go figure."

"What's happened to her, Rick? Has she gone nuts?"

"Seems fine to me."

"You can't just up and fire twelve hundred people—just like that!"

"That's kind of why I'm here."

"*What's* kind of why you're here?"

"Can she?"

"Can she what?"

"Can she fire twelve hundred people? I mean, legally?"

He paused.

"You're not going to quote me, are you?"

"Not unless you need the business."

He gestured to the waiting room, which now looked like a supermarket.

"Does it look like I need the business?"

"Okay, so off the record."

"All right then. Legally, she can do any damn thing she wants."

"Even to the tenured professors?"

"Tenure," he said, "has no standing in federal or state courts. It's a purely academic matter. Any professor—any administrator—can be fired for cause.

The myth that professors have complete job security is just that—it's a myth."

"So what happens if a tenured professor gets fired?"

"A lot of other professors get mad. And that's it."

"What can they do?"

"Well—" he shrugged.

"—the most damaging thing that they can do, as far as I know, is join together with other professors, and revoke the institution's accreditation. But you're talking academic nonsense now and it's far removed from the normal nonsense I deal with."

"So what are you going to do with all these people wanting to sue the university?"

"I'm going to take their names and addresses, and tell them to go home. Then I'm going to get drunk."

"Like I say—better get to it."

When Rick and Nina left the office, more cars were arriving, and the crowd was spilling out onto the sidewalk.

CHAPTER FIVE: THE BOARD

Half an hour later, they were in the board room, listening to the chairperson—whose name was Barbara Richardson—as she spoke to Lucinda Herndon about the impossibility of outsiders—them, that is, Nina and Rick—attending the meeting.

"You must realize that the events of the last hours have shocked us all, and that it is of the utmost urgency that we meet in *private* about this."

"I'm going to give a statement to Mr. Barnes," answered Lucinda Herndon. "He and I will go outside, and I can give it to him now. Or he can stay here, and I'll give it to all of you. You decide."

"Lucinda—"

"Come on then," the president said, rising, and looking at Rick and Nina, "This won't take long."

"No!"

Three people on the board said, "No" simultaneously.

"Lucinda, I beg you to be very cautious here. What you've done is—I don't know. Just—"

The chairwoman looked at Rick.

"Can we at least ask you, Mr. Barnes, to be discreet in what you write?"

"No," he answered. "I have to write the truth. It may be discreet; it may be indiscreet. But whatever it is, I have to write it."

There was silence in the room.

Finally, Barbara Richardson:

"All right. Then let the board meeting come to order. I, as I'm sure you all know, am Barbara Richardson, CEO of Adorn Cosmetics, based in Vicksburg. Lucinda, the floor is yours."

"Good," answered the president, rising.

She walked to the door of the room, opened it, and beckoned.

"You can bring these in now."

Several students appeared as though by magic, each carrying a large, black, cardboard box.

"Take them over there, to the end of the room. Put them behind the podium. And be sure there is chalk on the blackboard rail."

All of these things were done.

Lucinda Herndon then made her way—with some difficulty, since the chairs were close to the wall—to the front of the room. She stood behind the podium and tapped on the microphone. It was clearly off.

"Rick, Nina, can you hear me in the back of the room?"

They nodded.

"Good. Then we won't need the microphone."

And she began.

"At nine o'clock this morning, I personally fired the full-time faculty of this university. Nine hundred and eighty-six people were dismissed, including instructors, assistant professors, associate professors, and full professors. By mail, I informed three hundred and twenty-one administrators, including provosts, deans, vice presidents, etc., that their services were no longer required."

There was an audible gasp in the room.

"So. Are there any questions?"

Pause.

Barbara Richardson:

"Lucinda—you—you know you can't do this."

"It's done."

"No, but—but you simply can't."

"I have."

"But—but why?"

"Because they're useless. They're all useless."

"Is this a joke?"

"It was. It's going to cease to be. The joke is over. We can't afford it anymore."

"Lucinda, what are you talking about?"

"I'm talking about this. Here. Please pass copies of this article around."

She reached into one of the open black boxes beside the podium and pulled out several stapled copies of what was clearly an academic article of some sort. The Board, Nina found herself thinking, reacted like a class of dutiful college students as the papers were passed around.

"Does everyone have a copy?"

Everyone in the room nodded.

"Very well. I'm going to read aloud."

She read the following:

"The conclusion Bersani draws from this aesthetic desire to present the ruins of meaning is neither historicizing nor culturally prognostic. He explains the immobilized act of the consumption of art as a form of libidinal investment. Since one of the effects of being aesthetically immobilized is a sudden feeling of self-containment, the rhetors of impoverished art all experience their immersion into themselves. They adopt libidinal investment of egos that enjoy the situation when signification collapses. Because this situation revives the moment of narcissistic self-containment that once dominated the ontogenetic period before the acquisition of language, the driving force behind both comprehension and reception is simply a suspension of signification. The degree zero then is the form of art not entirely taken either by its questioning the authority or by being preoccupied by its own breakdown."

There was silence for a time.

"That," she went on, "is part of a book written by one of our full professors of English, Dr. Charles Altieri. The book's title is *Aesthetics and Politics in the Work of Pierre Bourdieu.* Now—"

She looked at Rick:

"Mr. Barnes?"

"Yes?"

"How many people write full-time for *The Gazette*?"

"Fourteen."

"Who is the best of them?"

"I am."

"What do you make of the prose I just read to you?"

"Gibberish."

"Thank you, dear. Actually, it's post-structuralism. What would *The Gazette* pay for it?"

"Nothing."

"Why?"

"Because it's gibberish."

"Do you know what we paid for it, dear?"

"No."

"Anybody? Anyone want to know what we paid for a book of this?"

Silence.

"One hundred and three thousand dollars."

There was another gasp, and a voice from the far end of the table could be heard whispering:

"Damn."

Then Lucinda Herndon once again:

"This is not counting Professor Altieri's travel expenses, of course, both to Corsica, where he lived— at our expense—while writing the book, and Rome, where he attended three conferences, during which various chapters of the book were given as papers. Professor Altieri taught no classes for us during that time, since he was on sabbatical.

The same voice again:

"Damn."

Lucinda Herndon leaned forward on the podium.

And then she screamed:

"I'm sick of this, and you should be too! We're all being robbed!"

Then she rocked back on her feet, stood straight, and simply glared at every single face sitting around the table.

No one said a thing.

All Nina could hear was the faint tapping of Rick's app, as he wrote what was being said.

And she knew, sending it directly to the newspaper.

Which, she also knew, would send it directly to every other paper in the country.

Lucinda Herndon, having successfully cowed everyone in the room, simply began to go through the articles that had been piled in the box nearest to her.

"'Romance, Sleep, and the Errors of the Rhyming Poem, by Arcadno'. No one has ever taught 'The Rhyming Poem.' Not at this university. Not at any university."

"'Sir Orfeo's Kunstkammer'. No one has ever taught 'Sir Orfeo's Kunstkammer' at this university. Nor at any university."

"'The Wallace Manuscript of the Siege at San Quentin.' No one at this university has ever taught, or heard of, 'The Wallace Manuscript'."

"How much did that article cost us?" asked someone.

"Sixty-eight thousand dollars. Dr. Silverberg wrote it. Along with three other articles. That is all he did last year. We paid him two hundred and four thousand dollars."

"And that's all he wrote?"

"No, Dr. Silverberg ranges out. He writes 'Copia Verborum,' and 'Milton in the Age of Fish.'"

"In the age of what?"

"Fish."

"Do you mean, like, real fish or—"

"I don't know."

Silence.

Then:

"That, ladies and gentlemen, is called 'Literary Research.' 'Literary Research' means that our faculty write things that no one else has said. This means that they are 'expanding the limits of the field.' The problem is that nothing they write has any relevance to the lives of our students. Or to the students' parents. Or anyone else. Here: let's pass on to the sciences. Dr. Orbison, on his work as a biologist:

"My research interests lie in the morphology of bryophytes. I'm currently conducting an investigation of the development of the cystolemic apparatus, as well as patterns of microtubules and micro fibulae, which are studied by techniques of immunofluorescence and transmitive microscopy."

"We pay," she continued, "eighty four thousand dollars a year for this research. Going on, here is Dr. Holliday on his research, also in biology:"

"My primary interests lie in the physiomorphology of decapods, especially burrowing thalassinoids. Special interest lies in osmoregulatory abilities and trophic ontogeny in the pineads. This work is carried out chiefly in Mexico, the Bahamas, Colombia, and the Cayman Islands."

A voice came from somewhere in the room:

"What do we pay for that?"

"We pay Dr. Holliday seventy-seven thousand dollars a year for that. Of course, some of that covers his travel expenses."

"What are burrowing thalassioids?"

"Shrimp."

"We pay him all that money to study shrimp?"

"Extinct shrimp."

"Pardon me?"

"The shrimp he studies are extinct. He's trying to find out why."

"My God."

Nina, despite herself, could not help whispering to Rick:

"Pulitzer."

But he simply continued to type.

And the president continued to speak.

"These are faculty, of course. Very few of them teach more than two courses per semester. Now to the administrators. The people without whom this magnificent university could not operate. I will not read their 'research interests,' because they have none. I will not talk about their teaching, as they do not teach. I will simply list the administrators who are currently being paid more than eighty thousand dollars per year, some of them much more.

The Provost.

The Vice Provost.

The Vice President for Administration and Finance.

The Executive Assistant to the Vice President for Administration and Finance.

The Assistant Vice President for Financial Services.

The Assistant Vice President for Administrative Services.

The Director of Operational Review.

The Associate Vice-Director for Operational and Contractual Services.

The Associate Director of Sponsored Programs, Finance Administration, and Compliance.

The Executive Associate to the Assistant Director of Information Distribution.

The Director of Auxiliary Services.

The Assistant Director of Auxiliary Services.

The Director of Academic Planning and Faculty Development.

The Assistant to the Director of Academic Planning and Faculty Development.

The Vice President for Academic Affairs.

The Vice President for Institutional Planning and Effectiveness.

The Associate Vice President for Institutional Planning and Effectiveness.

The Dean of the Department of Special Services Programs."

She paused.

"I could go on. There are a hundred and sixteen more of them. None of them do anything. Let me say this again, so that you understand it."

She paused again.

"None of them do anything."

"But, Lucinda—"

"Tom, in every office in this university, there is one woman who knows how things work. Registration, grade transferring, enrollment, adding and dropping— the true administrative needs of a university. One woman in each office. She is generally about forty years old, and she knows the answer to every question, having worked here all of her professional life, and being both resourceful and clever. This woman is generally paid forty thousand dollars a year. She and her equally clever and equally underpaid and underappreciated colleagues who are spread across the campus, accomplish all of the true, necessary, administrative work. They are, in fact, administrators. The rest, the ones I've just read to you are simply bureaucrats. They do nothing but go to meetings and eat chicken salad. The administrative bill for chicken salad alone is, for one school year, over one hundred thousand dollars. Mr. Barnes?"

"Yes?"

"Has your paper been trying all afternoon to contact these various offices?"

"Yes."

"How many administrators have you been able to contact?"

"Only one, I think."

"Why?"

"It's Friday."

"Thank you, Mr. Barnes. And, by the way, it's nice that somebody actually does work on Fridays."

Then she turned back to the blackboard.

"Now, I'm sure you're all asking yourselves, how much money are we talking about here? How much money are we going to save, yearly, by dismissing useless people. Well, I'll show you. Let's see what you get when you multiply 1263—the number of people fired—by one hundred thousand dollars a year, which is what most of them make."

Then she took a piece of chalk and wrote the figures:
1263
Then: times one thousand.
000
Then: times ten thousand
000
Then: times one hundred thousand
000
The figure on the board was:
126, 300,000,
"One hundred and twenty six million, three hundred thousand dollars. Per year. Every year. That is the amount of money we pay to people who do not teach, who perform no useful activity, who write things that no one will ever read, or who do experiments of no use to any current or future being on this planet."

She continued:

"Now, let us assume that similar figures apply to the top one hundred so called "research" institutions of this country. All of us together are wasting over one billion dollars per year. Every year."

The number hung there for a time.

Finally, a response came from the Chairman of the Board and from two other members, one whom the president had addressed as "Tom," and the other whose name plate was hidden. The two men were white-haired and pasty-faced.

"Lucinda," said the first of them, "No one questions that there are overages in the salary structure."

"There is, Oliver, *insanity* in the salary structure."

"All right. If that's what you choose to call it."

"That's what it is."

"Fine. But this is not the way to deal with it."

"No?"

"Of course not! You can't simply fire twelve hundred people!"

"Why not? Every week a major corporation or manufacturing company closes a factory and lays off just as many workers, including people who actually *work*. All that I'm doing is laying off people who do *not* work. At least not at anything sane or constructive."

Barbara Richardson.

"Lucinda, there are ways to bring about change."

"I believe I *have* brought about change."

"Yes, but at what cost?"

"Not cost. Savings. Over one-hundred million dollars. Do you have that much money to waste, Barbara?"

"But we should have been apprised!"

"You are being apprised."

Shakes of head.

Third white-haired man:

"President Herndon. This is a major research university."

"No, Tom, it used to be major research university fifty years ago.

Pause. Silence.

Barbara Richardson:

"Lucinda, we have agreements with foundations, research facilities all over the world."

"We certainly do, Barbara. I've been in touch with many of them, and it heartens me to know of their existence. I've simply told The Carnegie Foundation that we no longer have the funds to pay for Professor Olbive's research into extinct, burrowing shrimp. But that they are quite at liberty to take on his salary if they so choose. We will not begrudge them the glory of his discoveries. He and they can go down with Galileo and Jonas Salk as great minds of modern times. We will know about the motion of the planets; we will eliminate polio; and we will know what happened to these damned shrimp a million years ago—and the Carnegie Foundation will get the credit! It will only cost them, for the next five years, about five million dollars."

She paused.

Then, leaning forward, she said:

"But, Barbara, *we* can't afford it!"

Silence around the Board Room.

"And *you* can't afford it; and the students' parents, many of whom are mortgaging their homes so their children can come here and be educated, can't afford it; and the people of this state, who are paying us tax money so that we can do our jobs as educators, *can't afford it!*"

She shouted the last lines.

No one said anything for a while. Then, more quietly, the president went on.

"I am not curtailing anyone's freedom of speech. I am simply refusing to pay for what they say, especially when it's drivel. Absolute drivel."

"Lucinda—"

"Yes, Barbara?"

"Lucinda, these articles you've read. These research interests—of course, I can't understand them. I'll be the first to admit that. But I'm not supposed to understand them. These professors are experts in their fields. They're writing above my head."

Lucinda Herndon, at that, took the wooden podium from the table, and set it on the floor. She then sat down, sighed, and was silent for a time, nodding her head.

Finally she said, quietly:

"And that is it. That is the soul of it. Thank you for putting it so well, Barbara. I could not have done so. Perhaps my husband could have. He saw it beginning, you know, though it had never grown to the thing it is now. I wish he were here. I wish he were here to speak to all of you, because I'm not sure I'm capable. And it's so important. So, so important."

Again, she was silent for a time.

Finally, she said, quietly:

"Because you can't understand what they say, you think that they are somehow smarter than you are. But that is not true. Because they write in their own invented jargon, you think they are saying things infinitely wise. But that is not true, either. They say, 'morphological cytophormai,' and you think 'wisdom'."

She shrugged.

"When all it is, is garbage. In reality, they're just con artists, pulling off one of the greatest scams in history. Not since the French Revolution has such a useless class of people been treated with so much respect and given so much money. The only difference is that the French aristocrats dressed better."

She leaned forward:

"They're villains, Barbara. They're the bad guys. Our entire educational system is a shambles. Our middle school students don't know anything; our high school students don't know anything. And we blame the poor teachers. While all the time the 'best and brightest' of us, or at least the best paid, the most coddled—rather than inspiring us, rather than showing us the real magic in mathematics and literature and poetry—rather than giving actual models to the teachers and students and parents—they're flying off to hotels in San Francisco, where they can talk about 'the libidinal investment of collapsed signification'."

Then, with a shake of her head:

"They're frauds, Barbara. Frauds."

Then, to everyone else in the room:

"And they're fired."

She got up from the table, walked around it, and resumed her original seat.

After a time, Barbara Richardson said:

"We've all been touched by your passion, Lucinda. None of us, I know, myself certainly, realized the depth of your feelings on these matters. But you must realize the difficulty, the near impossibility, of the situation you've put the Board in. If you had consulted us, if we could have formed some kind of fact-finding committee—"

Silence.

Then:

"Lucinda, there is still time to reconsider this move. We could point out that it was a kind of 'shock therapy,' designed to help us actually assess where the university stands at this point in time, where there are areas for growth, where we need perhaps to cut back. We could—"

"No," said Lucinda Herndon.

Silence.

After a time, Barbara Richardson said:

"Well. You don't leave the Board much choice."

"You have two choices," the President answered.

"Then—we have heard your positions. I think now I must ask you—and our visitors—to leave the room. You understand that we will be voting on your dismissal."

"I understand."

"Then, if the three of you would—"

"I need to say something."

That voice came from someone who had not yet spoken.

"You all know me. I'm Pete Stockton."

The man had a huge handlebar mustache. His voice was deep, mellow, slow, like a clean north wind with stars sprinkled through it. As for the man himself, his face was like tinfoil, except brown instead of silver. Every line in that face was a washed out gulley in some cattle spread. He had slicked back hair, the color of real tinfoil and not brown tinfoil, and his eyes, if the lights had been turned out in the room and the shades drawn, would have sparkled and mean-glittered enough for all to read by.

"This president," he growled, "has fired more than twelve hundred people without consulting one damned person on this board. She could have formed committees; she could have done studies; she could have included the faculty in this thing; she could have included the Provost; she could have alerted the media. But instead, she just went off on her own and did it. Now we're sitting here with the Associated Press reporting every word of this meeting to the entire goddamned world—twelve hundred faculty and administrators out of a job—and all because this lady decided, completely on her own, to carry out this *vision* of hers.

He paused. No one would have dared say anything.

"Now. You all know that I give a sizeable amount of money to this institution every year. But if you support this woman, right now, in plain view of everybody—*I will double that contribution!"*

There was a huge *whooshing* sound as all of the air seemed, at once, to escape from the room.

But Peter Stockton merely continued:

"I've been on this board for ten years, and this is the first goddamned thing I've heard that's made a lick of sense."

He looked around the table, from face to face to face, then said:

"Moreover, I can assure you that I'm not alone in my feelings about this. I have a group of friends. We mostly started in oil and gas, but we've branched out over the years, and we dabble in a good many things at the present time. Information System Designs, Land Development...those kinds of things. And I can promise you this: if you support this lady and clean the polecats off of this beautiful campus, we will *all* double our contributions. Fire her and you won't get a nickel from any of us!"

The stare went around again.

"Also—you've been reading about this proposed bypass that either is or isn't going to get built north of town. It isn't going to get built because me and my friends now own that land. Not too many people know that, but they will. President Herndon—"

She nodded back.

"President Herndon, if you do, in fact, carry through with this, that fifty acres of land is yours!"

"Oh, my God!"

Nina had no idea who said "Oh, my God!"

It could have been anyone at the table.

"And my friends and I will build for you whatever buildings you want on it. They're all yours. You want dormitories, we'll build you dormitories. You want classrooms, for real teachers and not these imposters, we'll build you classrooms. The money we have available for this project—and I'm not talking a hundred million dollars, ma'am; I'm talking *real* money—is yours. We're having some problems with enrollment, I read. It's down a bit."

"Yes, Peter, it is," replied Lucinda.

"What do you foresee will happen to enrollment, if these good folks on the board here support you, and you get to carry out your full plans for this university?"

"It will double."

More shock from around the table.

"Lucinda—"

This from Barbara Richardson.

"—Lucinda, did you say "double?""

"Yes."

"But that can't happen."

"Of course, it can happen."

"But—by when?"

"Tomorrow."

"What?"

"Tomorrow. Our enrollment will double by tomorrow."

"Are you joking?"

"No."

"How can it double by tomorrow?"

"It will double tomorrow because of the story that Mr. Barnes is, even as we speak, sending to his paper, and which is being run on the Associated Press. Because of this story, the enrollment will double. And it will keep on growing."

"Good," said Peter Stockton. "Lucinda, I have no idea how you plan to double the enrollment of this university—"

"We will," she interrupted him, "take the vast amounts of money that we have been wasting on useless people and useless projects, and use it to educate the students who have entrusted us with it."

"All right then."

"We will, by the way, be the first institution actually to do that. And so our enrollment will more than double. It will, in fact, be whatever we want it to be."

"How many new students are you expecting, come next fall?"

"Let's say ten thousand. We'll cap it at that right now."

"All right. You have my word, Lucinda, that you will have classroom space and dormitory space for those folks. And for their teachers."

"Thank you, Peter."

All of the rest of the Board, Nina found herself musing, now resembled the disciples from Leonardo DaVinci's *The Last Supper*:   mute, insignificant, watching something they did not understand at all, but uniformly certain that it was pretty important, and that they had not heard the last of it.

"Now," said Peter Stockton, addressing the Board, "while you folks make your decision, Lucinda and I and Mr. Barnes and Ms. Bannister are going to find some place to have a cup of coffee."

Once they were out in the hall, the president spoke to Stockton:

"The last year has, I'm sure, been a difficult one for you, Peter. What with Maggie's death—"

"Yes, it's been tough. I miss her a lot."

"I know you do. We all miss her."

"But you went through that with Thomas."

"Yes. It gets easier. It's never the same. But it gets easier. Here. Let's go in here. The coffee is abominable. But the machines do at least work."

They contributed quarters and the occasional dollar bill, a process that seemed ludicrous in light of the past discussion. But somehow they were able to find four cups of coffee, get cream for it, stir it, and sit at a red vinyl plastic table beneath a huge television screen that was showing a game show.

Other than the four of them, the snack bar was deserted.

Peter Stockton smiled at Rick and said:

"I like your newspaper, Mr. Barnes."

"Thank you."

"There are only two things wrong with it."

"Those being?"

"Well, of course, it's too damned liberal."

"I know. We get that a lot."

"And the Friday crossword puzzle."

"Yeah. It's a hard one."

"I can do all the others. Monday I do in about ten minutes. But that Friday one, man, it's a bear."

"It's from *The New York Times*."

"Well, that would explain it. Explain the liberal thing, too."

"Yeah. Sorry about both problems."

"Probably not a lot you can do about either one. Ms. Bannister, it's an honor to be around you. Your Lissie movement took a lot of guts. I can see why you're a friend of Lucinda here."

The president smiled at Nina, then said:

"Nina is more important in this matter than she knows. I suppose I can tell you this now, Nina."

"Tell me what?"

"All of this plan was simply something in thin air. I wasn't certain I'd have the courage to do it. I saw myself as just one single person, and a woman at that. Then I saw the production of *Lysistrata* in Bay St. Lucy. I re-read the play. I was able to find tapes of your comments from Washington. And I said to myself, yes, it can be done. It simply takes guts. So I said, 'I will bring her here. I will see her again, and, if she's here standing by me—I can do anything.'"

For a time Nina knew nothing to say. Then:

"I'm very moved, Lucinda, that you think of me that way. But I just—"

"I know. It seems frightening. But don't worry. The worst is in the past."

Peter Stockton smiled:

"I believe she's right, Ms. Bannister. Now you may not believe this to look at me—rough old cowhand that I am—but I was once a student here. Lucinda's husband was my history teacher. I loved history. And do you know what Machiavelli said was the hardest thing for a Prince to do?"

"No, I don't."

"To change the order of things."

"Peter," said the President, "was one of my husband's best students."

"And he was a great history teacher," said Peter Stockton. "He made it come alive."

"He had talked with you about going to graduate school."

"Almost did, but other things got in the way. Maggie was pregnant, and the oil thing presented itself. One thing led to another—"

"—and you got rich."

He smiled.

"I got fortunate."

"That's one way to look at it, I suppose, but—oh, here's Barbara!"

And they were, in fact, joined in the snack bar by Barbara Richardson, who looked as out of place among vinyl chairs as she would have among paper plates or cheap shirts. She pulled a chair up, looked at it distrustfully, and sat down in it.

"Barbara!" exclaimed the President. "Please have some coffee. It's a dollar and a quarter, but, I'm sure, if we all put our change together—oh, and by the way, Barbara, I love your tan!"

Barbara Richardson managed a half smile.

"Vacation time in the Azores. It's one of the perks of never having been married—except to one's work. I don't have a husband to lug around. But to more important things: Lucinda, the Board has decided not to take action against you at this time."

"Wonderful! How good of them!"

"They have asked me to put certain questions to you—for our own information, you understand."

"Of course."

"Then, from a practical standpoint, Lucinda, how are our classes going to be taught? The semester begins this coming Wednesday!"

"We'll hire new teachers. Better ones."

"How are you going to find these people? And when?"

"I'm going to hire them this afternoon. By…what time is it now?"

"Ten thirty."

"By one o'clock, the contracts will have been signed."

"By whom?"

"Good teachers."

"I just—"

"Trust me."

"But what about the administrators?"

"One fifteen."

"What?"

"The administrators will have been replaced by one fifteen."

"Lucinda, we're going to get sued! Massively, collectively, sued!"

"No Barbara, we *should* have been sued in the past, for swindling honest people out of literally billions of dollars. If we could survive being criminals for decades, we can certainly survive being honest for a few hours."

"All right. Mr. Stockton?"

"Yes, Ms. Richardson?"

"The Board wishes to convey to you their thanks for your upcoming donation."

"You tell them it's my pleasure."

"The donation did not, of course, contribute to our final decision."

"Of course not. My understanding then is that President Herndon is not fired?"

"That's true. The Board is simply not taking action."

"When might the Board take action?"

"I don't know. Our next meeting is in October."

"So, essentially, if this thing works, you're going to say you were with her all along; and if it blows up in our faces and she really is crazy, you're going to fire her ass."

"I really can't—"

"That's the best we can expect," said Stockton. "By October, Lucinda, you'll have the land and I'll be putting up the buildings. If they fire you, you can damn sure come to work for me!"

"Can I," asked Rick, leaning forward over the ketchup and mustard jars, "have a statement for *The Gazette*?"

"Yes," said Barbara Richardson, taking out a sheet a paper: Please write, 'Although the Board of Regents regrets any inconvenience and temporary personal difficulty caused by the present necessary downsizing, we wish to assure all of the university's continued commitment to excellence in higher education.'"

"That's it?"

"Yes."

"Okay. I'm sending it now."

And he did.

"Well," said Peter Stockton, standing up, "I have a good deal of business to get to. I'm excited. I like building things."

"I must go also," said the Chairperson, dusting herself off as well as possible.

Lucinda Herndon turned in her chair and looked at Nina and Rick:

"Mr. Barnes, I believe you know where the Old Gymnasium is?"

"Yes."

"Why don't you meet me there in fifteen minutes? There will be another meeting, and you may wish to add to your developing story."

"What meeting is it?"

"Let it be a surprise. Just be there, and be ready to write. Nina, the meeting will be important for you, too. It will, I hope, affect your future. So—good by for now, but I'll see both of you in little more than an hour."

And, so saying, she left them.

They sat, as though stunned, for what seemed a great deal of time but probably was not.

Then Rick looked up, as though glimpsing a vision in the sky.

"Omigod."

"What is it, Rick?"

Only then did she notice the large television screen above and behind her.

"That's the faculty!"

"Where?"

"There. On TV."

And it was.

It was the big game hunter professor whom she had noticed before, who had introduced Lucinda Herndon to the faculty—now standing in front of a podium, preparing to read a statement.

"What do you think they're going to do, Rick?"

He shrugged.

"Dunno."

"Will they go on strike?"

"They can't go on strike; they're fired. They don't have anything to strike from. They don't—"

But he was interrupted by the professor on the screen beginning to speak:

"The Faculty has just emerged from a lengthy discussion of events that have only recently transpired. I am authorized to say that we, as a faculty, are united in expressing our deep concern. That is all that I can say at this time."

And he walked away from the podium.

"They didn't do anything," said Nina.

"No, they didn't."

Rick's cell phone whirred:

"Hey, Barnes here."

"This is Penn Robinson."

"What's up, boss?"

"You're doing great! There are stories going out all over the country—hell, all over the world—with your name attached. And, of course, with ours. Some of the stuff is damned good, too. I didn't know you could write that well."

"Thanks."

"So you're telling me that the Board is actually supporting this?"

"No. But they're not 'not supporting it.' They had the choice of firing Herndon or giving away—oh, three or four hundred million dollars. And they had to make that choice right in front of me and the world. And so, decisive people that they are, they decided it might be better just to go to tonight's cocktail party, and see which way the wind blows."

"And the university just got fifty acres of land?"

"Yes."

"And enough buildings for ten thousand new students?"

"Yes."

"Where are these students going to come from?"

"Don't know."

"And the university has gotten all these things because?"

"Because they fired the faculty and administration."

"We're all going crazy."

"Roger that, boss."

"Did you see the faculty announcement on TV?"

"Yeah, Nina and I just saw it."

"They didn't do anything!"

"No, they didn't."

"Okay, I want you to hook up with Sanderson. He just finished covering the faculty meeting. I want him to get his story to you so you can wire it to AP."

"Where is he?"

"Where are you?"

"We're at the student center now."

"Where are you going next?"

"Old gym. There's another meeting of some kind that the president wants me to cover."

"What meeting?"

"Don't know."

"Okay, I'll call Sanderson. He'll meet you in front of the gym."

"Got it."

Cell phone shut.

It took them five minutes to reach what Nina assumed was the old gym, and at that point, they were approached by a tall sandy-haired reporter, whom she soon learned was Sanderson.

He ran to meet them. *He had a kind of wild-eyed look about him,* she thought, *as though he'd covered both the Hindenburg disaster and the sinking of the Lusitania in the same day—one in the morning after breakfast, the other in the afternoon before tea.*

"You're not going to believe it!" he said.

"We haven't believed anything about any of this yet; why start now? By the way, this is Nina Bannister, who, we've just learned, is the inspiration behind all of this."

"Pleased to meet you," said Sanderson. "What the hell did you start?"

"I didn't know," said Nina, "that I'd started anything. Until a few minutes ago."

They pulled two wooden benches together so that they faced each other.

"Okay, you ready to take this down?"

"Shoot. What happened in the faculty meeting?"

"Well, two fistfights happened."

"What?"

"There were two fist fights."

"Among the faculty?"

"That's right."

"Why?"

Sanderson leaned forward:

"Because the faculty hate each other."

"So who had the fights?"

"The first one happened about twenty-five minutes into the meeting, and was between someone in the Environmental Studies Department and someone in the Gay Lesbian and Transgender Studies Department. Several punches were thrown, and I think somebody got a broken nose, although I couldn't get close enough to tell. Anyway, the police came and took somebody away."

"Who did they take away?"

"Dr. Judith Anderson."

"Wait a minute: this fight involved a woman?"

"Well, with the Gay Lesbian and Transgender Studies Department—"

"Yeah, I know. But the second one—"

"That was clearly two women."

"From—"

"Aaahhh, here it is: The Department of Celtic Ethnography and the Department of Neurokinetic-Forensic Studies."

"What happened?"

"I don't know. But they just kept talking at once, Rick! Finally, they were standing up and yelling at each other. The only thing they could decide on, was that they needed more time, and it was completely inappropriate for them to act without setting up fact-finding committees. But since a quorum of faculty members wasn't available—"

"It's Friday."

"Yeah, that. Since a quorum of faculty members wasn't available, they'd have to do a mass email to all full-time faculty members and get a 'Sense of the Faculty' so they could propose a motion."

"When will that happen?'

"Some time next month, apparently, because, given the time of the semester it is, they all have research conferences to go to."

"Next month?"

"Yes."

"But they're fired!" Nina said.

Sanderson nodded:

"Someone kept saying that—and that person was told to sit down, but wouldn't—and then the first fight broke out. And then the police came."

"Sanderson, surely they must have adopted some kind of resolution!"

"They have one resolution that they decided to email to the faculty. Actually, they wrote three resolutions, but they couldn't agree on the first two."

"What were the first two?"

"The first one was an appeal to the American Association of University Professors, demanding censure of the president and revocation of accreditation."

"Did that get voted on?"

"No. Five professors got up and said they shouldn't do it."

"Why not?"

"Because revocation of accreditation would damage their chances of getting their research published."

"But they're fired! They're fired!"

"Well, that's what the second resolution dealt with."

"So what was the second resolution?"

"It was a query asking for more information and clarification of language in the president's original message to the faculty."

"Clarification of language? She said *fired*. I was there, goddamn it! She just said, 'You're all fired!'"

"Apparently 'The Sense of The Faculty'—and, of course, there can't really be a 'Sense of the Faculty' until two-thirds of the faculty is there—"

"Which there will never be because they're goddamned fired!"

"—the 'Sense of the Faculty' is that the president's message can be understood in a number of ways, and that it would be imprudent for the Faculty Senate—which is the only Faculty organ empowered to impose censure—to act hastily, without linguistic clarification from the Office of The Provost."

"But there is no more Office of the Provost!"

"Somebody pointed that out, and somebody else said the Provost was in Hattiesburg at a conference, and somebody else said, 'Doing what?' And then the lawyer came."

"What lawyer?"

"The one the president sent over with the retirement packages."

"What retirement packages?"

"The ones she's offering to all faculty who are willing to sign by tomorrow and clean out their offices by Monday."

Sanderson breathed deeply. There were just too many words that had to be said in the last three hours, to fit in the lungs of a skinny reporter.

He acted as though he were preparing for the steeplechase.

Finally he was ready.

"Most of these faculty, you understand, have been working here more than ten years. There aren't many young full-time faculty. When an old full-time faculty member croaks, he gets replaced by three part-timers, who teach twice the number of courses for one-tenth the salary."

"But the part-timers don't do any research."

"Which is the other good thing about them. But most of the full-time faculty have been making a hundred and fifty thousand dollars a year or so, with a tenth of it going into TEA CEAF."

"Which is what?" asked Nina.

"The teacher retirement system. So all of these people have at least a hundred and fifty thousand dollars socked away in teacher retirement, which the president offered, over the next five years, to match, at thirty-thousand dollars a year. So they'll have three hundred thousand dollars apiece. They'll be on easy street for the rest of their lives,"

"So how," asked Nina, "did they faculty react to this?"

They started yelling at each other again, and…"

"Don't worry about it now," said Barnes. "We've got another meeting to go to."

And they did.

CHAPTER SIX: BEES IN SPRINGTIME

The Old Gymnasium immediately became one of Nina's favorite places on campus. It harkened back in her mind to Bay St. Lucy, when, on winter nights, the town would pack in to see the basketball team.

She and Rick made their way in through the double doors and were struck by the sight of unkempt people lying about like street litter, stretched across benches in the concession area, huddled in corners, sitting facing computers at make-shift desks they'd pulled up.

"Who are these people?" asked Rick.

"I know who they are! I recognize some of them from Nick's, yesterday. They're all adjunct faculty members."

"Hi, Nina!"

"Oh, hi Tyra! Rick, this is Tyra. I met her yesterday. Get her to tell you about the frog."

"What frog?"

"The one that can perform oral sex. Except he—"

Rick interrupted:

"Maybe later. But just look! Look at all the part-timers!"

And it was true. The gym was filling.

Tyra smiled weakly, looked out over the sea of faces milling around like ants, and said softly:

"They anon with hundreds and with thousands trooping came attended: all access was thronged, the gates and porches wide, but chief the spacious hall thick swarmed, as bees in spring time..."

"What's that from?" Nina asked. "I love it, but I don't remember it."

"Milton. *Paradise Lost*. We're all going to be fired, aren't we?"

"I don't know, Tyra. Tyra, do you...do you teach *Paradise Lost*?"

She shook her head.

"No, I teach remedial writing. Part-timers aren't allowed to teach literature. I love Milton though. She fired the whole faculty this morning, I heard."

"Yes, she did."

"And the administration, too. Look—there she is!"

Lucinda Herndon entered the gym from the north portal, walked under the backboard and basket, crossed the free-throw line, and approached half court, where a platform had been set up, with several metal chairs and a microphone.

The entire gym fell silent.

"Farewell happy fields," whispered Tyra, "We're all fired. Well...be it so, since she who now is Sovran can dispose and bid what shall be right. Oh, God, she's getting ready to talk. The President. One who brings a mind not to be changed by place or time."

The microphone wheezed and screamed. A maintenance worker appeared like some helpful rabbit in a Disney movie, tinkered with it, tapped it with his finger, made it wheeze and scream again, shrugged, and left it to Lucinda Herndon who, probably like Satan in the mind of Tyra if not the assembled throng, spoke:

"This morning," she said, "the faculty and administration chose to accept early retirement. I would now like to ask you to run the university in their place."

There was first absolute silence, then a kind of general hubbub; then atrophied physical movement— erratic head shaking, limb quivering, foot and leg discontrol—then incoherent questions, and then questions somewhat coherent but incomplete and second-language sounding.

"Could you?"

"I—"

"Did I—"

"What?"

It soon became clear that Lucinda Herndon knew every part-timer in the hall, and referred to them by first name, an impossible task since, not only had nobody else at the university bothered to learn the identity of even one part-time professor, most were convinced that no part-time professor even had a first name.

"I would like for all of you to meet your colleague Thomas Swinton. Dr. Swinton has his doctorate from Princeton. He teaches two sections of remedial German for us. Did you have a question for me, Dr. Swinton?"

"I—I—"

"Oh. Well, then let me repeat myself. The full-time faculty and administration accepted early retirement this morning. I would now like to ask all of you to run the university in their place."

"But—but I—"

"I know. This is difficult. Let's begin by doing this: everyone waiting at the doors of both ends of the gymnasium, please come in now!"

And this loosed into the gymnasium, a stream of creatures which might have come from Milton, whom Nina resolved—in deference to Tyra—to read more thoroughly. There were people in orange uniforms carrying black boxes, the kind Lucinda Herndon had brought to the Board meeting. There were photographers, at least twenty or more, some of them with outlandish hair and Rolling Stones outfits, others, she assumed from Fox News and Affiliates, wearing grey suits with little American Flags in the lapels—all of them carrying gigantic cameras, many of them kneeling, some trying to get as high up on chairs as possible, the others trying to get as low down close to the floor as possible, all trying to get as close to Lucinda Herndon as possible.

"All right."

Those two words had the effect of slowing everything down slightly. Certainly not stopping it, but of changing from 78 rpm to 33 1/3 rpm—that is, things began to go slower, which was certainly good, but they became more dreamlike, and continued to go around in circles.

"All right, let me do this first."

So saying, she reached into one of the Black Boxes.

"These are contracts," she said. "There are approximately a thousand of them. I'd like you to sign them. You have been making two thousand dollars a course, and you were limited to two courses per semester. The university didn't want to let you teach more because we would've had to pay for your health care and benefits. You will now be making five thousand dollars a course and we'll ask you to teach eight to ten courses per year. That's forty to fifty thousand dollars a year, but, of course, we will pay your health care and benefits. Is that clear to everyone?"

There was a moment of silence.

Then everyone stood up exactly at the same time and started clapping.

The clapping got generally louder, but it was interrupted in its general increase because it had to be interrupted by the hugging and the crying and the daubing of the eyes and the shaking of the heads and all of the general emotional let going that would have happened in the Joads' migrant camp in California if somebody important had driven through yelling, "Steaks and jobs for everybody!"

"Sit down, please. Be quiet."

Finally, everybody did, but it was with difficulty.

There was general jubilation and unbelief.

The faculty—because now, obviously, they weren't the part-timers anymore, but were going to be the *faculty*—were leaning forward like the first night audience of *Psycho*, smiling the vacant smile of the suddenly insane, waiting eagerly for the next murder.

"We will be receiving twenty new ten-story buildings next year as a reward for firing—sorry, offering early retirement—to our old faculty and administration. Ten of those are for you."

This time a gasp. A general gasp.

"There will be room for a thousand teaching faculty in the most modern apartments Peter Stockton and his friends can manage. Rent free. There will be cafeterias in all of the buildings and you can have every meal there that you want, also for free. Where *you* are, the university is. Where *you* are, learning takes place. And I want you here working with our students, and not at the Drake Hotel in San Francisco getting drunk on martinis and talking about structuralism."

Finally, someone actually stood up and asked a coherent question:

"How can you afford to double our pay, give us benefits, and give us free room and board?"

"We can afford it because the people who took early retirement made more than two hundred and sixty million dollars a year and did little to no actual work, leaving you to do most of the teaching. Doubling your salaries, housing you and feeding you, as well as giving you the benefits you deserve, will cost sixty million dollars a year. We will actually be making a huge savings. We will pass that savings on to you and to our students. Whom we will finally—finally—begin to teach."

More clapping.

When the clapping was finally over, the president got the floor again.

The gym was packed now; there was also chaos going on outside. Nina could hear sirens, helicopters—and could even see people's faces pressed against the high windows up over the top section.

"Sit down and be quiet!" the President ordered.

And, gradually, everybody did.

"We need to hire an administration."

"What is happening?" Rick asked.

"Why do you think," Nina answered, "that I would begin to know that now?"

"Here are the duties," Lucinda Herndon pronounced, "of the Provost. This comes, by the way, from the University Handbook:"

1. Fostering inter-faculty collaboration in the sciences, social sciences, and humanities.
2. Fostering interfaculty collaboration in the sciences, social sciences, and humanities.
3. Improving university performance in building a diverse pipeline of scholars and in developing scholars at all stages of the academic career ladder.
4. Advancing university-wide approaches to compliance and research policy.
5. Oversight and coordination of international activities.
6. Support for University cultural and artistic entities and projects.
7. Oversight of academic and administrative computing initiatives undertaken by the University's Central Administration Information Technology group.
8. Oversight of activities pertaining to intellectual property, technology transfer,

research collaborations with industry, and trademark licensing.

"How many of you can foster, foster, improve, advance, oversee, and support? Oh, by the way, the previous provost was paid $475,000 dollars per year for fostering, coordinating, and overseeing. In the new pay scale, the job offers a thousand dollars a year. But we still need someone to do it, I suppose. Now, who thinks you can do these things?"

Every hand in the audience went up.

"How many of you play golf?"

Most of the hands went down.

"All right, of those volunteers remaining, how many like chicken salad?"

Only two hands remained.

"One of you is the Provost. The other assists the Provost in doing all of these things and thus becomes the Assistant Provost. Two people associate themselves with the Assistant Provost and thus become the two Associates to the Assistant Provost. All of these jobs originally paid from $250,000 to $300,000 per year, and we are now offering five hundred dollars. There are 123 administrative contracts up here waiting for signatures, all of them paying $200 to $800 a year for jobs that require no training, no special ability, and no physical work. I'd like them all signed before you leave. Now, I have today been sternly admonished for banning useless bureaucracy and studies disguised as *research* from this campus. To that, I can only quote Emerson in *The American Scholar*. He said:

'The deafness, the stone-blind custom, the overgrown error you behold, is there only by sufferance—by your sufferance. See it to be a lie, and you have already dealt it a death blow.'

She looked around. Then, she said:

"The necessity of what has been passing for research, the necessity of more than one hundred bureaucrats doing nothing and taking our money for it––these things are lies. And they're dead. Don't be afraid of them anymore."

Finally:

"Emerson also said: 'Free should the scholar be. Free and brave.' All right. I know you're brave, because I know what you've had to endure. Now you are free. Go and teach."

And she walked away from the microphone.

No one moved for a second.

Then almost everybody moved.

There was a mad dash for the gym floor and for the contracts.

Tyra remained motionless for a moment, simply shaking her head in disbelief.

Rick looked her straight in the face and said:

"Tyra, the president has just fired the whole full-time faculty. She now wants you and the rest of the part-timers to replace them, for about a tenth of the money. Will you do it, or will you boycott classes in support of the full-timers?"

Tyra responded: "We care about the full-time faculty just as much as they have always cared about us. Most of them don't even know our names. To hell with them!"

"Thank you."

"You're welcome. Now let's go get our contracts!"

They stood up and made their way down the stairs as well as they could, trying to make sense of the general pandemonium going on around them.

They were on the gym floor now. So was everybody else, milling, crying, or laughing. They were in an adjunct river after the research dam had broken and was being washed away.

Everyone, obviously, was trying to talk to Lucinda Herndon, but she broke away from a mob of photographers and made her way over to Nina, into whose ear she whispered:

"Do you know where the administration building is?"

Nina nodded, saying:

"I was there yesterday. It's the most depressing place I've ever seen."

"Well, it's about to change. My office is on the second floor, room 224. If you and Mr. Barnes will meet me there in twenty minutes, I need to offer you a job, a big job."

"You mean teaching English?"

"No, dear. I mean helping me lead this revolution."

CHAPTER SEVEN: A JOB OFFER

The Administration Building was filling up with people not knowing what was going on. There were ex-adjunct faculty who now believed themselves to be administrators, and were rushing to take possession of their offices. There were real (former?) administrators who either were cleaning out their offices or barricading them, vowing to fight what they saw as an insane decision or a huge joke.

Shouts could be heard coming from the various corridors and floating down the staircases.

Policemen had begun to arrive and were walking the halls, nervously communicating with each other on walkie-talkies.

Nina and Rick entered the main floor and turned left. Office of the Vice Provost; this was Mathieson, one of the administrators to whom Nina had spoken the previous day. He peered at them through the glass wall for an instant or so, standing, completely motionless, beside what had some hours before been his desk. Then he smiled and beckoned for them to come in.

"Shall we go in?" asked Nina

"It's a story."

"Why do you think so, Rick?"

"Because from now on, everything on this campus is a story."

They tried the door and found it locked.

The man inside threw up his hands and made the little counter-clockwise finger gesture indicating insanity.

Then, smiling, he ambled around the desk and opened the door.

"Come in, come in. What can I do for you?"

It was a question he must have asked a thousand times in his life, and enjoyed asking it, his tanned face dotted like a brown map with laugh lines and crows feet that betokened a constant and easy smile.

He hardly seemed aware of how out of place the question seemed now, when clearly there was very little he could do for the two of them, or for anybody else, now or at any other time. Ever.

Because he was fired.

"Dean Matheson, I'm Rick Barnes of *The Gazette*."

"Ah yes! Well, you're becoming a celebrity! I've heard a great deal about you today!"

"I'm sorry," he said, "about that."

"Don't be! You're just doing your job. I think this is a big story we have going on here."

"Yes, sir, it is."

"Then I'll ask you again, what may I do for you?"

"I wanted to get some comments from you."

"Oh, you mean for publication? For print?"

"Yes, sir."

He shook his head.

"I don't know that I have much to say."

"Are you going to contest your firing?"

He shook his head, slowly.

"No. No, I've never tried to go against the university. I—all of us, you know—serve at the pleasure of the President."

There was for five seconds, six hours of uncomfortable silence.

"Do you know, sir, if most of your colleagues are reacting in the same way?"

He shrugged.

"I've only been able to reach a few people. Some of them are very angry."

"Of course."

"Some are just still in shock."

"That's understandable."

"This is, of course, unprecedented."

"Yes, sir."

"When I first heard about it—actually I was mowing the lawn. I was supposed to be with the provost in Hattiesburg, at a conference of college and university administrators. But something came up. I had to cancel at the last minute."

He chuckled.

"And so I was here. Mowing the lawn. If you can believe that. Well, my wife came out and told me that she'd heard it over the radio. And I said, 'What did you hear?' and she answered, 'They're firing everyone, Charles! They're firing everyone!' I ran over and held her—of course, she was crying, and I asked, 'Are they firing me too, Claire?' and she had her face buried in my chest and just kept nodding and nodding and I remember thinking, "This can't be true. It can't be true. There has to be some kind of horrible misunderstanding."

"Yes, sir."

"I had no idea when she said, '*They*'re firing everyone,' what she meant by *they*. That's such a horrible word, isn't it? It's so impersonal. Such horrible things have been done by *they*. I could only think of wars and mass killings, and the specter of screaming women running out of buildings, shouting 'They're killing everyone! They're killing everyone!' No, this *they* was so frigid, so anatomically catastrophic."

He looked up, then shrugged again.

"For a moment, I thought it must be some kind of joke and then I realized—no—things would never be right again."

He waited for a time. Then:

"Of course, there were phone calls, speculations, outraged people running here and there and everywhere. The wives met and tried to support each other. I know Claire had several people over. I wandered about helplessly, not knowing if I should dress up and go to campus, or just wait where I was for some kind of instructions. But the common thread running through all of it was that the president had somehow gone insane. There was simply shock and astonishment that one person had the power to inflict such total destruction. Such total, personal destruction. So we thought, 'She's lost her mind.' We kept telling each other that. But then we heard the news of the Board's—well—the Board's non-decision. They did nothing at all. Which means, I assume, that we are still dismissed."

He could not, for a while, continue.

Then:

"The hardest part of all of it, of course, is what the president apparently said about our—well, our uselessness."

"I don't think," Rick said quietly, "that she was talking about you, sir."

Although Nina knew that he was exactly who she was talking about.

"No, I suppose not. But when you're told early in your life that you're useless, then you do something to make yourself useful. But when it comes late, and you look back, and, think you've done a pretty good job, and been a good colleague and provider—well, you just—"

He shook his head.

"I shall miss dealing with the students. I've always like being around them. We always seemed to have something to talk about."

He thought for a while, then stood, and then extended his hand:

"I bet you folks have work to do. The whole country is taking an interest, I hear. Firing 1200 people—an entire faculty, an entire administration. It must be newsworthy."

"Yes, sir. It is."

"Of course. Well, as for my official statement, Mr. Barnes, are you ready?"

"Go ahead, sir."

"'I regret the actions of the President, but I support her, as I always have, and will support any course of action that the Board deems proper for the well-being of the University and the students of our state.' How's that?"

"Thank you, sir."

Then the two of them left.

They walked down a corridor that led deeper into the building, looking for a stairway that might take them up to the second floor, when they passed another office, large and familiar to Nina.

Now she remembered. It was the provost's office.

Inside it stood two women, both bending over a desk, then looking up at them. They gazed at them much as Matheson had done, but no smiles crept across their faces.

They were women who looked quite similar: business-suited, trim of build, one with flaming red hair, and the other with hair much the color of Lucinda

Herndon's, except pulled straight back and tied in a braid that hung almost to her waist.

They continued to stare.

Nina felt instinctively that the two of them should have kept going. But they did not.

Like deer in headlights, they stood looking back at them, dumb show mutual zoo gazers at the Administrative Hall for Wildlife and Spectators. Neither side knowing which was the wildlife, which the spectators.

Finally, the mime ended with both women, as though set loose by the same instinct, walking in an almost run step to the glass door and sliding it open.

The woman with the flaming red hair stepped through the wall—or where the wall should have been, had the door not been there—studied them for a long five seconds, looking them up and down.

"This is my husband's office. He's Charles Iverson, the provost. I'm his wife, Amy Iverson. What are you doing here?"

They said nothing.

"Are you part-time faculty? Because you're not coming in here, do you understand that? Now get the hell away from here!"

"Ma'am," Rick stammered.

"Don't *ma'am* me! I told you to get the hell away from here!"

"We're just—"

"You're just trying to come in here and take what doesn't belong to you! My husband is a top administrator at this university, and he's going to stay one. We will fight this insanity, do you understand? She can't do this!"

"We're not part-time faculty," said Rick, calmly. "I'm a newspaperman. I'm Rick Barnes of *The Gazette.*"

There was a momentary pause.

Then the woman who had identified herself as Amy Iverson surged past the braid wearer and lunged straight at Rick, stopping only inches from his face, as though halted like a bulldog by a leash two inches long enough.

"I remember you now, you creep! You're Barnes, the reporter! You write vicious things about my husband, and about the university. And you have for years."

"I just write—"

"You were in our house once, years ago, when Charles and I first came here. And you even had us over. Then you just turned against him!"

Rick seemed at a complete loss for words.

"You creep!"

Then he stepped back, almost involuntarily, so that he was pinned against the wall by both women who— seeming to forget Nina—started showering him with obscenities, hatred glowing in their eyes.

"You creep! Are you going to win some sort of prize for this? Is this a game for you, or what? Do you get paid for costing us our livelihoods? How much? How much do they pay you per word?"

Then a policeman appeared at the other end of the corridor.

"What's going on here?"

"Nothing," said Rick.

The policeman, a huge black man with guns and shining badges and handcuffs and red and blue and tan insignia and nightsticks and six feet two of body, walked quickly toward them, saying:

"Well, something sure seems to be going on! You can be heard all over the building!"

They simply stood there, pursing their lips and shaking their heads.

Finally:

"There was an argument," said Braidwoman, holding the palm of her hand toward the policeman and pushing it repeatedly forward into the air, against nothing, as though it were actually repelling an unpleasant fact, which, if pushed far enough away from her, would simply disappear.

"There was an argument, and we let our tempers get out of hand."

"I'll say you did."

And then came the buzzing of his walkie-talkie.

Still glaring at us, he unhooked it from his belt, swung it to his ear, and barked into it.

"Yeah. Yeah, I'll be there."

Then, to the four of them:

"I'm assuming this is over, right?"

Nods around the group.

"All right. You can all go."

Five minutes later, the two of them were sitting in Lucinda Herndon's office.

"Lucy," said Nina, "this is all incredible. I had no idea—"

"I know, Nina. It's not what you expected."

"It's not what anybody expected. People are in shock."

"They'll get over it. Mr. Barnes, you're covering all of these events admirably."

"Thank you."

"But now I must ask you to consider writing another story."

"All right. Shoot."

"I can't. Not quite yet. Not until I get a confirmation."

"A confirmation about what? And from whom?"

"About a job. And from Nina."

Nina sat forward:

"What?"

"I'm about to offer you a job, Nina."

"But you have offered me a job. I'm supposed to be teaching an English course."

"And you will, if you wish to."

"If I wish to?"

"Yes, you may choose to decline."

"Why would I do that?"

"Because you might not have time."

"I'm sorry, but I'm not understanding any of this."

"Perhaps I can clarify it. I actually invited you to come to Ellerton because I need you for a much larger job than teaching one course. I couldn't describe the job to you before because—well, because you knew nothing about the events of this morning."

"If you had told me about them, Lucy, I wouldn't have believed them."

"And you would probably have stayed in Bay St. Lucy."

"Well, since you mention it…"

"Of course. And that's perfectly understandable. But you must at least let me tell you of the job. Because I honestly believe it to be crucial to my vision of the new Ellerton."

"All right, Lucinda. But I just don't see how I can be a part of any of this. So many people fired, so much anger…"

"The anger will dissolve. All of the people released will have money to live on—a good deal of money— for the rest of their lives. If they wish to spend their remaining years researching extinct shrimp, so be it. But I'm much more interested in hiring now than firing. And that's where you come in."

"Where?"

"I want you to find teachers for me."

"But you just hired more than two hundred adjuncts."

"And they will teach a great many of our courses. Their numbers will be supplemented, though, by Golden Age teachers. And you will be head of The Ellerton Golden Age Teaching Project."

"I don't understand."

"It's not that difficult, Nina. Think of it this way. If you ask most people—people from any profession, any age—who their favorite teacher of all time was, almost all of them will have one they want to talk about. Mizz Suggs from the fourth grade. Or Coach Daniels. Or that great high school history teacher who just seemed to make everything come alive, and whose fifty-minute class seemed to be over only minutes after it began."

"Yes, I guess that's true."

"Of course, it's true. And the thing is, it's only one per person. Nobody was ever lucky enough to have two great teachers. Only one. The other thirty or forty get divided into a group that were all right and hard-working, but not magic—and another few who weren't worth shooting and never should have been in the classroom to begin with."

"Yes. I've known some of them, too."

"Nina, there are right now, even as we are speaking, a thousand or more wonderful high school teachers—teachers of all subjects, from English to biology to mathematics to history—who are in good health, and simply living the life of a retired teacher. I want you to find those people and bring them here."

"But how would I do that?"

"You will do it, and you can do it, because you're Nina Bannister. You *are* one of those people. And I'm betting that if asked right now, just because of your experience with thirty years in the classroom and in the principal's office—you could name me at least fifty wonderful teachers whom you have known, have worked with, have observed, have met in various conferences—and who are no longer teaching. Who are, in short, being completely wasted."

Nina, almost involuntarily, began thinking.

And it was true.

Felicia Harrison, who had taught with her for years in Bay St. Lucy.

What an inspiring English teacher.

She made it, according to every student, come alive.

Bill Meyer from history.

Tom Congdon from over in Hattiesburg.

More came to her mind.

And more.

She interrupted her own reverie to ask:

"All right, I know a few. But I'm not sure if some of them are even still alive. I'm especially not sure if they'd want to go back into teaching."

Lucinda Herndon shook her head and said:

"They probably would not wish to go back into high school teaching, dealing with the ever present wild and unruly student who has to be sent to the office. But this would be college teaching, teaching in an environment most high school teachers were never allowed entry into. Students who listened, and colleagues who were all creative, who could all learn from each other."

"All right, a lot of them might be interested in something like that."

"Of course, they would. We would pay each one forty thousand dollars a year, which they would receive in addition to teacher retirement. They would live here on campus, just as the people who were adjuncts are going to live, in the comfortable apartments that Peter Stockton and his friends are going to be building for us. All of their meals—if they should choose to take them on campus—would be free. Tell them: come and teach for three years, and you can put into the bank another hundred thousand dollars with which to supplement your retirement. Now tell me, Nina: is that not an attractive proposal?"

She realized there was but one answer.

"Yes."

"Could you not use another hundred thousand to live on?"

"Of course I could. But I still don't see how I'm going to find enough teachers who are really great at their job. Yes, I know a few, remember a few. But as for the rest—"

But Lucinda Herndon simply smiled and nodded.

"You go into towns in Mississippi and simply hold your finger in the air. Think, Nina: if any stranger were simply to go into the library in Bay St. Lucy and ask one of the older librarians: who is the best high school teacher Bay St. Lucy ever had, what would be the immediate answer?"

Nina mused for a time and then said, softly:

"Me."

"Of course. And there are *you's* all over the state. Their names are not collected in any one journal or printed on any one plaque; for they have become part of the town's mythology. We will pay you, Nina, and pay you well, to travel around the state and find these people. Find them and bring them back here. You would, in short, be doing research. But it would not be blathering nonsense and it would not be called structuralism. It would be mining for gold, that presently is hidden and doing no good."

Silence for a time.

"I—"

"Think about it, Nina. Think about it."

She said she would.

And then the two of them left.

CHAPTER EIGHT: A CABIN IN THE WOODS

They returned to the offices of *The Gazette* to find Penn Robinson standing in the door.

"Okay. It's all out of control."

That fact was made obvious by a casual pause to listen. A blue and white helicopter was flying low over head, the faces of photographers visible through the Plexiglas windshield. Sirens seemed to be going off everywhere.

"The radio announcers keep going over the same figures, the same sentences. According to the AP, the nation's leading one hundred largest universities are wasting more than a billion dollars a year on useless research and useless bureaucrats. Do you have any idea the effect that is having?"

"I can't imagine," Rick said.

Robinson shook his head.

"Well, let's just try to get at one thing at a time. The country is almost broke. We're having riots in the streets in New York and Chicago to protest Wall Street. People are out of jobs, losing their homes. Whole cities are going bankrupt. And now: a billion dollars a year. A billion dollars a year!"

The helicopter continued to circle, getting shots of the part-time faculty who, as they were exiting the gymnasium, were waving hand-painted posters that said:

Down with the full-time faculty!

Nina could make out on the side of the helicopter the words: *ABC News*.

"It's going to get worse," Rick said.

"You better believe it's going to get worse," Robinson countered. "There are apparently demonstrations against *The University of Waste* being planned on campuses all over the country."

"Which campuses?"

"University of Idaho, in Boise."

"That figures," he said. "Conservative West."

"University of Wyoming."

"Yep."

"University of Colorado."

"Figures."

"Harvard."

"Oh, God."

"And people are coming here. Jesus, are they coming here. By the busloads."

"Who's coming here?"

"Everybody. Reporters, TV types, politicians, but mostly parents. They have no idea what's going on. They can't find out anything any other way: they have no idea if the university will even *exist* by Monday."

"What are the politicians saying, boss?"

Robinson shook his head.

"Obviously, the most conservative Republicans love it. The Tea Party guys have been ranting about pin-headed academics for years. Two Republican senators have publically endorsed Herndon's *bold initiative* and are exhorting college presidents to take similar actions."

"What about the Democrats?"

"They don't know *what* to do. Their first instinct was to be outraged over the firing of two thousand people. But this isn't like the firing of two thousand actual working men and women, union members, truck drivers, steamfitters—no, these are academics whom nobody—*nobody*—sympathizes with or likes. And not only that, it's *bureaucrats*. It's a paradox. The people who just got fired are all liberals, so you'd think the Democrats would support them. But they all make a hundred thousand dollars a year—except for people like the provost, who make four hundred thousand—do no physical work, and summer in Europe. In other words, they *live* like Republicans. So the Democrats don't know what the hell to say about them."

He paused, then continued:

"No one likes these people, you know? They have no organized basis of support. Who's going to man the barricades backing 'University English Professors for Extinct Shrimp?' And 'The Association of Vice Directors and Assistant Curriculum Planners' is hardly the Teamsters' Union."

The editor shook his head and said:

"On the other hand, they're not going to take this lying down. The administrators are flying back to campus as fast as they can. The American Association of University Professors is already threatening the University's accreditation. The more sane faculty members are organizing. I don't know what will happen, but something will, and probably within a few hours."

"So what do you want us to do, boss?"

"Get out of town. You need to lie low for a while. Everybody's looking for you, Rick, either because they love you or because they hate you. You can't report the story for a while because you've *become* the story...which can't be allowed to happen. So, is there somewhere you can go, at least for a few hours, until this begins to die down?"

"Yes, I think so.

"All right. Take the station's van. I don't even want you going back to your place to get your car."

"Okay, thanks, boss. I'm going to take Nina to—"

"I don't want to know. Just get out of here."

And they did.

On the way out of town, neither of them spoke. Finally, Rick said:

"I'm sorry I took his offer so quickly, Nina. I should have asked you if you wanted to come."

"That's all right. And by the way, where else am I going to go? Everybody who hates the president—or you—now hates me."

"It's too bad it's happened that way."

"It *always* seems to happen that way. I look forward to a few days of rest and relaxation, and then all hell can break loose. It's just that when it breaks loose, it tends to do so in so many different ways. Why don't the authors who seem to be creating me at least try to write the same book twice, so I'll know what's coming?"

She shook her head and said:

"No, that's just the way it is. So where are we going?"

"Some friends and I have a hunting/fishing cabin."

"Sounds perfect."

And it was.

And that worried her.

For a time, they simply drove.

It was a nice drive, and within a few miles, it put the sirens and the helicopters and the police cars all behind them. The radio emitted a bit of elevator music which, mixed with the murmur of the engine, seemed to have the same lulling effect that windshield wipers do during a long trip in rain.

The chain restaurants and filling stations came more sparsely. They started up a few hills that became gradually more wooded. Finally, there were just pines and blue sky, the sun behind them becoming multi-colored as its rays deflected through whatever layers of waste and garbage in the atmosphere made it look golden and magical.

Rick told her he'd bought the cabin several years ago as a kind of time-share venture with a co-worker or two, his lawyer friend and a computer salesman who'd since moved away. For the first year or two, he explained, the group had spent a good deal of time in it, four or five of them having a boys night out occasionally, playing poker and drinking beer until late on Friday nights, and canoeing off the hangover at whatever time on Saturday they chose to rise.

They stopped at a grocery store some miles beyond the city limits. Rick went inside and bought dinner for them—ground beef for stroganoff and a bottle of red wine.

After about twenty minutes more, they turned off the main road and started meandering the van over a rutted gravel lane that led through thick firs and balsams, getting just a glance here and there of the lake.

The cabin looked inviting. There was a pier leading out to the green glass-still lake, the surface of which was dotted only by a few double-bump bullfrog heads and up-jutting logs that had once been willow trees. The swing and flier-chairs still sat placidly in the screened-in porch.

"Well, we're here."

"This is nice, Rick."

"The guys and I don't come out here nearly as much as we used to. Somehow we just can't bear the thought of getting rid of it."

They got out of the van.

The lake, she noted, had begun to make its late afternoon/evening sounds. There were no longer the tree frogs and humming mosquitoes of mid-summer evenings, but the crows still circled and cawed, and some kind of animal—maybe a deer—could be heard crunching quietly over the fallen leaves and decomposing twigs.

They crossed the porch, which overlooked the lake. Rick unlocked the door and they went inside.

He took the groceries into the kitchen, saying over his shoulder:

"Would you open a window?"

"Sure."

The cabin still had the musty smell of a place infrequently occupied, but, as she opened the window behind a green leather sofa, she could feel cool, pine-cone-scented air float in.

"I might go out on the porch," she said, "and sit on that swing."

"Good idea. Can I bring you a cup of coffee? We always keep some here."

"That would be great."

She sat down on the swing, slipped her shoes off, and propped her bare feet on a wooden rail that surrounded the porch.

On the other side of the lake, a hundred yards or so away, a deer walked into a clearing. She could see him stop, raise his antlered-head that was somehow not-brown not-gray but the exact color of the whole surrounding forest, then lower his head and meander away.

After a few minutes, Rick joined her, and they rocked together, looking out across the water.

"You going to take the job Lucinda offered you?" he asked.

She sipped her cup of coffee and watched cream swirl in it.

"How did you know I wanted cream?" she asked, quietly.

"I don't know. I just did. I was right, wasn't I?"

"Yes."

"So, are you going to take the job?"

"I don't know. It's scary."

"Why is it scary?"

"Because she may be insane."

"Well, there's that."

"And even if she isn't insane, half of the people in town hate her now."

"That's true."

"And then of course there's—"

"What?"

She sipped again.

The coffee was perfect.

But, for that matter, the lake was perfect.

"I just—my home is in Bay St. Lucy."

He nodded.

"Yeah. Anybody special there?"

"Everybody there is special. It's my home. Has been all my life. Mine and Frank's."

"How long has Frank been gone, Nina?"

"Ten years."

"I see."

"Look," she said.

"What?"

"The deer is back."

"Is that the same one or a different one?"

"The first one," she continued, "was a buck. Horns. This one is the doe."

"So I guess they belong together."

"Yes."

"Would be unnatural for them not to be."

She did not answer.

"Yeah."

They swung for a time.

"What do you think will happen, Rick?"

He shook his head.

"I don't know. I keep thinking, there's no way she's going to pull this off. And yet, she keeps pulling it off. Then I think of you, going around the state, rounding up the great teachers, the really fantastic ones, and bringing them all here..."

"I'm not sure I could do that."

"Of course, you could. Not many people could. But *you* could."

"Why me? Why could *I* and not somebody else?"

"I don't know. But you could."

They were silent for a time.

"Okay, so we know all about me," she said. "What about you? Who is Rick Barnes?"

He smiled:

"All right. I was born here and went to a high school. I was kind of a loner. I got okay grades, but wasn't much of an athlete, so had a mediocre social life. There were a few girls, but no one special."

"And there never has been?"

"No, it just never happened."

His cell phone rang.

"Hey."

"Barnes?"

"Yeah?"

"Okay, the faculty and administration are striking back."

"That figures."

"The Provost has just arrived back in town from a conference, on a private jet from Vicksburg. A lot of other suits are pouring in. They've been networking with other faculty and *research interests*, whatever those are. But there's a lot of them, and there's big, big money at stake here. Herndon may be crazy, but when she talks about billions of dollars, she's right on. The hundred or so biggest universities have budgets bigger than the hundred or so biggest corporations."

"So what's happening?"

"Damage control as much as possible. And then, they've called a meeting."

"What kind of meeting?"

"Parents and students. Tonight, eight o'clock."

"Where?"

"The stadium."

"The stadium?"

"Rick, busloads of people have been pouring in all afternoon. Nobody knows what's going on. They'll have more than five thousand parents here, some praising Herndon, some cursing her. Once you get the media, the ACLU, the AAUP—the damned AAA for all I know—anyway, the place will be filled."

"What are these suits going to say?"

"What can they say? The whole thing is a horrible mistake. The President is—"

"Crazy?"

"They don't want to say that. But they're going to say the Board had no idea what she meant to do—"

"—which is a lie."

"—and basically told her not to do it."

"—which is a damned lie."

"Then they're going to replace Herndon with the Provost."

"Where's the President now?"

"Nobody knows. Nobody can get a statement out of her."

"So this is basically over, right?"

"I don't know. Billions of dollars? Herndon's got some big politicos on her side, too. And a lot of just plain simple people out there who're asking if this money is really being wasted, and, if so, why. Oh, and one more thing—"

"Yeah?"

"You gotta get here for this meeting, Rick. This whole thing is your baby."

"I know."

"So my advice is to stay wherever you are for now, and lie low for a few hours. Then make your way back into town. See you at the stadium."

"Okay, boss."

Then he hung up.

"You heard, Nina?"

She nodded.

"You have a loud cell phone."

"I have to go back into town and cover that meeting."

"I know."

"You can stay out here if you want to. It may get ugly."

"I can get ugly too."

He smiled.

"I guess I haven't seen that side of you."

"Be glad."

"Well. We have a couple of hours. Then let's make our stroganoff and we're off, back into town. Want to go out on the pier and fish a little?"

She shook her head:

"What I want to do is lie down on the bed for an hour or so and just try to rest."

"I can understand that."

"These last hours…"

"Yeah, I know. So. I'll do the fishing. Maybe get a catfish or two. You take it easy."

"Thanks."

He went outside, and, after a time, she could hear what she assumed to be fishing gear rattling on the porch.

She lay down on the small, but neatly made bed in a corner of the living room.

She stared at the ceiling.

She *was* tired. So much had happened since this morning. The brief meeting with Lucy, following her to Grierson Hall, the shocking and impossible announcement, the board meeting, the adjunct meeting, the offer of this incredible job—a job that no one had ever been offered before—

—all of these things had happened.

But they were not the problem, of course.

They were not the things that mattered.

Other things had happened.

Rick had happened.

Why was being around him so easy?

The feelings that she thought might be arising in her no longer existed. Had no longer existed.

Frank.

Frank?

Where was Frank when she needed him?

And then it was not Frank who came to talk to her, but Nina herself.

And Nina said to her:

Frank is dead. You may see him again, in another life. But for now, he is dead.

Then she thought of those feelings.

Were they dead?

Then, finally, she dozed off to sleep.

When she awoke, the window was open. Had it been open the whole time? Probably.

The world had darkened, gradually.

Propped on an elbow, she could see porch lights begin to come on in cabins to the right and left, bordering the lake. She got to her feet, went to the kitchen, and saw that Rick had started the water boiling for the stroganoff noodles.

In a skillet to the side, the beef browned with sauce simmering with it softly. The kitchen was in a kind of purple half-light that came just before darkness.

"What time is it?" she asked, a bit groggily.

"Six-fifteen. We need to leave here in about half an hour. I'm not sure I want to get back into town until after dark."

"You're joking, I guess."

He shook his head:

"No."

The lake in near-darkness; a huge orange moon coming up over the black tree line—

He dished up the stroganoff and poured a glass of wine for each of them.

They ate on the porch.

"I hope you take the job," he said.

"Yeah."

"I know you think it would be scary, but it would be nice to have you in town."

"That's the scary part, Rick."

"Am I that scary?"

"Yes."

"Why? What about me is scary?"

"Nothing. And that's what frightens me."

They ate, drank their wine, and said nothing more.

CHAPTER NINE: THE STADIUM

There was something sentimental, she mused, about *driving into town on a Friday night and seeing the lights of the football stadium.* Something intimate about the enclosed darkness of the car, the glittering evening star in the west, where the sky was still a kind of darker than royal, royal blue—and the lights themselves announcing like a huge carnival that *our town is showing itself tonight!*

They drove straight to *The Gazette* office to find Penn Robinson standing in the door, wearing a suit. She thought it seemed strange to see him wearing a suit. It was a dark brown suit, covering a light yellow shirt bisected by a dark brown tie, not quite—disastrously, fashion-wise—the same color of the suit.

Making him look ridiculous.

He waved them into his inner sanctum, the same room where they'd been several hours before.

She noticed, as they walked past the various alcoves, booths, and cubicles, a great may new faces.

Reporters.

Important reporters, who were talking non-stop on cell phones, and had no time to look up as they passed.

Robinson closed the door behind them.

The room was in semi-darkness, probably the way he wanted it.

"All hell is breaking loose," he said.

"So, is she fired?"

"Not officially, yet. The Board is going to make that announcement tonight. I think it will be in a press conference outside the stadium. Then the Chairman of the Board of Regents will introduce the Provost as the new president, and they'll all speak publically to the parents—and God knows who else—inside the stadium. It's like I told you on the phone, Rick: they're going to say it was a huge mistake. The Board was misquoted at their meeting today. By you. And they're going to imply that the president has lost her marbles."

"Where," asked Nina, "is she?"

"Still in the Residence."

"Has anybody been able to get to see her?"

He shook his head.

"It's like a police state over there. There have been all kinds of threats against her. Bomb threats, even. I mean, you just can't fire twelve hundred people and go walking around like nothing's happening."

"Have you tried to call her?" I asked.

"Sure. Everybody's trying to get through. The campus police aren't letting anybody in. My guess is they're following orders by the Board and the Provost. Tomorrow, they're probably going to tell us she's under some kind of medication. Treatment for stress, that kind of thing. She's probably going crazy over there, but we'll never get through to her."

Then Nina remembered.

"I have a phone number," she said. "Lucinda gave it to me this morning. She said I could always reach her at this number, no matter what else was happening."

She took out her cell phone, found the card with the private number that Lucinda Herndon had given her this morning, and dialed it.

The president answered immediately.

"Nina!" she said, gleefully. "How wonderful to hear from you! Isn't it a marvelous day!"

Robinson and Barnes stared open-mouthed, first at each other, then at Nina.

"Nina," the president continued, "we're going to be unveiling some incredible programs in the next two or three hours. I want Rick to publicize them to the world."

"She is," Robinson whispered, "absolutely insane. Doesn't she know she's going to be fired in the next two or three hours?"

"I wouldn't bet on it," said Rick, quietly.

"What?"

"Nothing. It's just—this woman—I just wouldn't bet on it."

"Lucinda," Nina continued on the cell phone, "are you all right?"

"Of course! Why do you ask?"

"It's just that—at the meeting tonight—"

"And isn't that a lovely idea! I do so appreciate the outgoing faculty and the provost for getting such a nice crowd together. It's predominantly parents, you know. I so look forward to talking with them."

Robinson through up his hands and whispered, almost in desperation:

"They're not going to let her out of the Residence! She's gone completely out of her mind!"

"Lucy," Nina continued, "we're getting word that the Provost—"

"Yes," they could all hear her say through the cell phone, "he's back in town. The dear man. Well, it's nice of him to come. We shall make him feel very welcome. The crowd will be appreciative. Now I must hang up, for there are so many other things to prepare!"

"Lucy—"

"Good bye, dear!"

She hung up.

Penn Robinson shrugged his shoulders.

"Crazy as a loon."

"So, what do you want me to do now, boss?"

"It's like this afternoon. You're still the damned story. Every reporter in town wants to talk to you, to get you to admit you made up the whole thing."

"That's what the Board is saying, is it?"

"That's it. And they're going to say it publically."

They finally reached the stadium and made their way through Gate 24. The thing Nina was to remember most vividly was, with all the sounds, the blaring bullhorns, the clattering of horses' hooves, the tumult of usually normal voices now getting louder and louder simply in an effort to be heard—with all these things, plus the helicopters roaring over the stadium, manned by police with spyglasses, reporters with laptops, and politicians with microphones—the thing she was to remember most vividly was thinking, "this is the State Fair on Opening Day, or it's the Biggest Game of the Year, or it's the World Series!" but without any fun attached, and with no food.

There were a few reporters, especially clustered around a large open area to the north of the stands, which was covered now with electric wires that matted over it like yellow, plastic-covered fibers of a huge electronic video spider's web. It was ringed by lights and suits, and more lights and suits, with policemen and national guardsmen.

A platform had been set up. Ringing this platform were the Board members. The Chairperson of the Board of Regents tapped once on the microphone, making it squawk successfully for silence:

"My name is Barbara Richardson. I serve as Chairperson of the Board of Regents. I want to make a few remarks to some of you, though our official statement will be made later, out in the stadium. At that time I shall apologize on behalf of the Board of Regents for the distressing, not to say frightening, events of today. Our hearts go out to the families of the faculty members and administrators whose lives have been shaken by this morning's announcements from the Office of the President."

She paused for a second, and then went on:

"We the Board of Directors heard the president's proposals for the first time at our ten o'clock meeting this morning. The rest of the board and I were shocked, as you may suppose. But out of our great respect for her, and for the memory of her honored husband, we decided rather than to act on a motion of immediate dismissal, we would plead with her simply to take no action for the remainder of the day—and week—while we were attempting to contact other leading figures of the university community, such as the Provost, Vice President for Daily Operations, Executive Chancellor, and others.

She paused to let that sink in.

A north wind freshened. It was becoming cooler, and the huge lights glared on the faces of the people ringed behind her, and standing just in front of the columns of the buildings.

"Unfortunately, our strategy failed. The President, for her part, did not allow us the time she had promised, but proceeded to hold a completely unauthorized meeting with our valued part-time faculty, whom she cruelly deceived. Now, in retrospect, it is clear what the duty of the board should have been. We should have relieved the President of her duties immediately and asked the Provost to assume her duties while a search was made to replace her. Failing to do so, we failed our entire university community, and other similar communities around the county. And for this we are so, so, sorry."

Finally, she said:

"Our only recourse, as we watched these sad and almost unbelievable events unfold, was to work through the university itself, and contact as many parents, as many members of the university community, as we could, and invite them here tonight—along with members of the local and national media, who have likewise been deceived—so that we could clarify, personally, the situation as it now stands. We will be doing this in a very few minutes. I would like now, though, before we proceed farther, to introduce the Provost of this university, Dr. Charles Iverson. I can announce now that Dr. Iverson will be assuming the duties of the President for the immediate future. Dr. Iverson?"

The Provost followed her to the microphone.

"I've just flown in from Vicksburg, and I may appear a bit haggard. But let me begin by saying how much I appreciate Barbara's comments, and how deeply grieved I am to be assuming duties which, as challenging as they are, will of course prove even more daunting because of the course of events today. I regret the comments that came from the Office of the President, and must say quickly and clearly: our faculty will continue in their present duties, as will our administration. Any *contracts* that have been forced upon them within the past hours are specious, and non-binding, as are any *retirement* agreements. I will, in the course of a very few minutes, be making these points clear to the parents of our students, who are, rightfully, almost in shock about the news of the firings of their children's teachers."

Short pause. Then:

If there is one good thing about this situation, it is that it affords me the opportunity to reconfirm to the entire academic community, to our students, to our parents, to the nation, and to the world, that this university has assumed gladly, is assuming, and will continue to assume its crucial role as a major research institution."

Another pause.

"What is such an institution? That question defies the simple answer, due in no short part because of the growing complexity of the world in which we live. But suffice to say, that it is a community of scholars living, interacting, working non-stop, on the cutting edge of all we know—on the cutting edge of medicine, or history, of literature. It is a community of minds pledged to the daunting—yes, sometime even the terrifying—task of extending forward the very boundaries of human existence. We have in our midst—and are extremely privileged to have gathered in our midst—a number of the greatest minds living, working, and writing, today. If we, as a community, as a group of administrators, can support, nourish, inspire these minds, then I can promise you, we *will* cure cancer!"

Applause from some people in the now-growing media crowd.

"And we *will* go not just to the moon, but Mars—and beyond!"

More applause.

"We will plumb the depths of the ocean, and unlock its mysteries. We will go to the very heart of the beginnings of life itself, as our partnership with the great Fermi Atomic Particle lab shows that we are already doing. Are there those who question the need for the human mind to be ever-probing? Of course. Are there those who ask for the immediate gratification of tangible proof, concerning the uses of their hard earned tax dollars? Of course, there are! There have always been the forces of anti-intellectualism. But because mankind has triumphed over those forces, we have the cameras that you are focusing on this podium today; we

have the automobiles which you have driven here; we
have the medicines that have prolonged and are
prolonging our very lives. And so, to those who
question the commitment of this great institution to the
cause of research, be it medical, agricultural, economic,
humanistic...I say *no*. No! We will never back away
from our challenge. *Never!*"

More applause.

"As far as the events that have transpired today, we
all deeply regret them. They have been brought about
by accusations of waste and of poor oversight. Of
course, we are concerned by such accusations. It is the
job of the highly-trained administrators of this
university to ferret out waste. We don't want it; we
shan't countenance it. If it exists, we will root it out.
This is the work that we are continually trying to do,
and we will never waver. Given that these regrettable
events have awakened public concern across the
country—yes, I'm sure you've all heard the talk shows—
—"

Laughter.

"—given that fact, I am personally organizing a fact-
finding committee, headed by myself, and augmented
by the Chancellor, Vice Chancellor, Director of Human
Resources, Director of Institutional Planning, and Vice
Director of The General Fund...to find out if there is
something truly behind these accusations, and do what
we can to stop them."

More applause.

"I also wish to stress this point. Yes, we are
committed to the vitally important world of research,
and to playing our part in that infinitely complex world.
But we are committed most of all—to our students."

Louder applause.

"Our research and our teaching—of those students, those precious students, those leaders of tomorrow—go hand in hand, and always shall go hand in hand."

Same level of applause.

"Finally, I must offer my most sincere apologies to a special group of those who have been misled by comments coming from the Executive Office. We shall, of course, be studying in weeks and months to come, ways to expand both the role and the compensation of one of our most valued resources: that is, our adjunct faculty. We could not get along without these folks, who help out those of us in the actual university community daily, in a wide variety of roles. Just give us time."

A pause. Then:

"It remains only for me to say how deeply disappointed, and angered I am at our local media outlets. The story that appeared in *The Gazette* this morning made it appear that the board, at least for a time, was supporting the actions of the president."

Upon hearing this Rick stepped forward and said, firmly:

"They did support her actions."

"That," said the provost, his voice rising, his face reddening, "is a lie!"

A hush fell over the crowd.

Nina, to her surprise, found herself taking Rick's hand.

How long had it been since she'd held a man's hand?

The provost:

"Mr. Barnes, you should be ashamed of yourself. You wanted to write a sensational story, and you did."

"I wanted to write the truth, which is what I have been doing all my life."

"You wanted your name *out there*. And it was. Stories by Rick Barnes, distributed to *the Associated Press*, running in *The New York Times*."

Rick took another step forward, taking Nina with him.

He and the provost were no more than five feet apart.

No one else in the crowd moved or spoke.

"Do you realize, Mr. Barnes, how many people have been cruelly deceived by your desire for sensational publicity?"

"The only deception involved is going on right now, and it's being perpetrated by you," replied Barnes.

"Again, sir, I tell you: that's a lie, it's a damned lie."

"Say that again, you son of a bitch, and you'll regret it," said Barnes.

"I already regret a great bit," countered the Provost. "I regret that I wasn't present at the meeting this morning to prevent this massive fraud you've perpetrated. But I can tell you, you won't get away with it. The university is taking two courses of action: first, we are demanding that *The Gazette* terminate your contract immediately."

Nina moved closer to Rick.

Her arm was around him now, and she found herself holding tightly.

She was trying to hold him back.

But failing.

His eyes were flashing, his breath heaving.

"Second, we are preparing a major lawsuit against the paper. It has acted irresponsibly and caused great suffering."

"It has done its job and so have I."

"What you have done is attract national publicity. What were you *attempting* to do, Mr. Barnes?"

And now the provost looked directly at Nina:

"Were you trying to impress your new girlfriend?"

Two flashbulbs went off.

Then Rick lunged forward:

"Uggghhh!"

He was out of Nina's grasp immediately, and before she could even scream, the two men were writhing on the ground, clawing at each other, their shoes kicking wildly and becoming entangled with the electric wires which seemed, like writhing snakes, to be everywhere.

Now everyone was screaming, or shouting, or cursing, or pushing forward, or pulling back.

Finally, several policemen had gotten Rick and the provost onto their feet, separated them, and cordoned them off, so that they could no longer see each other.

"Rick!"

Nina tried to reach him but could not.

Within five minutes order was restored.

Somehow, neither the provost nor the reporter who'd attacked him had sustained any major injury, although Rick was clearly giving away a great deal of height and weight to his huge adversary.

Rick's chin, Nina could see, was bleeding slightly.

He sat beside her on a straight chair, daubing at the scratch.

The press conference had broken up, with the group of suits and politicians threading their way toward the entrance to the field level, the provost among them.

An older police officer stood before Rick and addressed him:

"You all right, sir?"

Rick nodded.

"Yeah, I'm fine."

"I'm supposed to interrogate you."

"All right. Whatever."

"The people from the university are pretty mad."

"I'm pretty mad, too."

"They want me to arrest you and take you downtown."

"Can they order you to do that?"

"No, sir. I act on my own discretion."

"Did you see what happened?"

"Yes, sir. I was right there."

"Did you hear what he said?"

"Yes, sir."

"What would you have done?"

"Broken his jaw."

Rick shook his head.

"I'm not that good at fighting."

"Well, Mr. Barnes, next time you just ask me."

"Is the provost going in there to speak?"

"Yes, sir. Unfortunately, you didn't hurt him."

"You realize I have to cover the story."

"If that's what you have to do, Mr. Barnes, I'm not going to stop you. Just try to stay far away from the provost. Or anybody wearing a suit for that matter."

"All right. Thank you, officer."

"That's quite all right. And remember: next time you just ask me."

The officer left.

Within five minutes, they'd entered the stadium, and were making their way toward the top row.

"Are you all right, Rick?" Nina asked.

"Yeah, I'm fine. Sorry about that. I kind of lost control."

"Well, he was lying. We were both at the board meeting. We both know what they did. And didn't do," she said.

"Yes, he was lying."

"Do you think they'll really sue the paper?" Nina asked.

"I don't know."

"Everything he said was wrong. Vile and wrong," she said.

"Not everything."

"No?"

"No."

"So what did he say that was not vile and wrong?"

Rick smiled at her:

"He said you were my girlfriend."

They continued to climb.

The first thing that caught Nina's eye was a row of chestnut-brown horses stretched across the field, each horse seeming sixty feet tall or so, each one standing perfectly still, each one ridden by a soldier.

At precisely eight o'clock, a row of dignitaries paraded up onto the podium.

Barbara Richardson tapped the microphone, as she had done earlier in the press conference.

There was no sound, though.

The microphone was dead.

Then the lights in the stadium went out, and the Jumbotron—that is, the giant scoreboard above the North end zone stands—lit up.

And there, in full color, on a giant television, was Lucinda Herndon, dramatically swinging open the doors of the Residence veranda and sweeping forward, to a microphone set up just in front of the rose bushes.

"I don't believe this," whispered Rick.

"I want to thank," she said, beaming, "all of the parents and students who have come out this evening. I also want to thank Barbara Richardson, the esteemed chairperson of our Board of Regents, and Dr. Charles Iverson, who had until today, served us in the capacity of Provost. Please give them a hand."

Twenty thousand people in the stands applauded politely.

The stage in the center of the field was in complete darkness, and the microphones did not work.

You could see the forms that had once been dignitaries, and had now become shadows, remain absolutely motionless.

"Lucy, I love you," Nina whispered,

The President continued:

"Will you please watch the screen?"

Her image disappeared, and was replaced by that of a lush green meadow, dotted with trees and magnificent, ten-story, white buildings.

"What you see before you is a projection of the newest addition to the university. It will comprise fifty acres of land."

Ooooohhhs and aaaaahhhhs from the crowd.

"And there will be twenty new ten-story buildings, which will be used for classrooms, dormitory space, and living space for new faculty. The addition will be called "The Richardson Complex," in honor of the Chairperson of our Board of Regents, Barbara Richardson. Barbara—"

A spotlight shone straight on Barbara Richardson.

She smiled.

"Will you please wave to the crowd, Barbara?"

"If she waves—" Rick whispered.

Barbara Richardson waved.

"—then Herndon's won. I'll be damned."

The image of Lucinda Herndon reappeared on the screen.

"The second announcement is one that I make with mixed joy and regret. I did accept the early resignations of a number of our faculty and staff earlier today. That is the matter of regret. My joy though comes from the fact that, due to these early retirements plus a wonderful and unexpected gift from an anonymous group of donors, we will be able to cut tuition and fees for the following year at this university, plus the overall cost of attending school here, that is, books, food, lodging, etc.—costs which had amounted, as you know, to slightly under twenty-five thousand dollars per year—by *one half*!"

A gasp from the crowd.

"You have understood me correctly. You will only be paying one half of what you were paying last year."

And then cheering.

And then standing cheering.

Nina looked around. Men were hugging men, women were hugging each other—the very columns in the stadium seemed to be crying.

The chanting started:

Herndon! Herndon! Herndon!

Finally, it died down enough so that she could say:

"And now would you all join me in singing our National Anthem."

Everyone stood up.

Piped music began.

Ooww say can you see—

A hush. Soft voices singing. Cathedral like silence. Some tears coming now.

And the rockets red glaare!

The bombs...etc. etc.

Wild cheering beginning with—

Laaand of the freee!

—and complete and utter jubilation by the end of *braave!*

Then, for one last time, the beaming image of Lucinda Herndon in front of the wide veranda doors of the Residence, blowing a kiss and saying:

"Good night, everyone! And May God Bless!"

CHAPTER TEN: OYSTERS

"That's the most remarkable thing I've ever seen in my life," said Rick, rising from his seat.

Nina was about to answer—although it would have been difficult, given the melee that was going on around them—when she was approached by an undergraduate boy who wore a pony tail and had thick, black, horned-rim glasses. The boy bent low and said quietly:

"You're Ms. Nina Bannister?"

"Yes, I am."

"I'm one of President Herndon's aides. She said I was to locate you, and give you this letter."

"Thank you."

She opened the letter and read:

"Please join me for a late dinner after the meeting at the stadium. We'll have oysters! If you walk to the residence, just wait for me at the back entrance. I'll be there a bit after nine."

The letter was signed *Lucy*.

"Rick," she said, "do you want to come? I'm sure she means this for both of us."

"I don't think I can."

"Why not?"

"Well, Nina, there's something I've been meaning to ask you."

"What?"

'I'm not—I'm not sure. And I'm not really sure how to ask it. I need to walk for a time and think. But, why don't we do this: there's a wine bar on Hacker Street. President Herndon can tell you where it is; it's only three blocks from the residence. After your oysters, why don't you meet me there?"

"All right, Rick. Have a nice walk."

And think about what it is you want to ask me.

Because, she mused, *I already know what it is.*

What I don't know, is how I'm going to answer you.

Within only a few minutes, she had walked to the back entrance of the residence.

She sat on a porch swing and waited.

After a short time, Lucinda Herndon arrived.

"Nina! You could come!"

"Wouldn't have missed it, Lucy! Congratulations!"

"Thank you, dear. But what about Rick? How is he?"

"He's all right. Just a scuffle."

"What a horrible thing. That brute Iverson. I never thought such a thing would happen."

"I know, Lucinda, but the things he said before we got into the stadium—"

"Don't worry about those comments. A small cluster of unimportant reporters—after what happened in the stadium, he'll have to recant. So will Barbara. They'll be forced to say that they were *misinformed.*"

"So you've won?"

"Of course, I've won. I won the moment Peter Stockton opened his mouth this morning. Millions of dollars, maybe even more. Acres and acres of donated—that is, *free*—land? An immense cut in tuition rates. Nina, even as we're talking right now, four of our professors, all of whom were earlier in the day merely adjuncts, are planning a six-week study tour in Paris, combining language study, art history, music appreciation, and European history. This six-week trip—and there will be many more like it, trips all over the world—will be free. Free for up to a thousand students, each of whom merely needs to say 'I want to go.'"

"But how is that possible, Lucinda?"

"We're saving two hundred and sixty million dollars a year by laying off useless people. The trip I've just told you about costs $10,000 per student. Ten thousand times one thousand is ten million dollars. We're still a quarter of a billion dollars to the good. Now come. I hope you like oysters."

"I love oysters."

"Some sherry, followed by cold white wine?"

"I can be forced."

"Good. There is a small fire going inside, although it's probably too warm to warrant it. Still, it looks so nice. Now, let's go inside."

They entered the back of the Residence.

Fire burning, lights golden—it was like walking into a Christmas card.

"Please sit down, Nina. Here. We're by ourselves, I've given the staff the night off. So many people all day—I just felt the need for privacy."

They sat in giant green amoebas that served as chairs and were situated, at the present time, in position to engulf the fireplace-andirons after only a few more stages of growth.

Lucinda Herndon poured herself a glass of sherry and toasted:

"Well, then: to a marvelous day!"

"I'll have to go along with that, Lucinda. I have to ask, though: how was Peter Stockton able to get these building plans done in just a few hours?"

The president looked at Nina incredulously for a second, then laughed:

"Oh, of course, these are not the *exact* buildings! This is actually a picture of a development near Montclair, New Jersey. But it has trees, just as ours will, and it has buildings, as will ours."

"I should have known."

And then the two of them chatted for some minutes about things much less important than a revolution in how universities should be run. Finally, Lucinda said:

"Our oysters are in the dining room. Shall we go?"

Nina rose and followed her.

A few of the oysters had slithered down her throat when she asked:

"What do you think their next move will be?"

The president simply stared for a time.

"What next move?"

"Well, they're not going to simply take this."

"Who?"

"The faculty. The administrators."

"The faculty *are* the administrators now, as they were for the most part throughout the history of this institution. "Director of Curriculum Development!" For God's sake, as though it were not the faculty's job to develop curriculum!"

"I mean, the old faculty. The old administrators. There are so many of them."

"There *were* so many of them. Far, far too many. It's shocking, when one looks back on it."

"They're not going to just leave, are they?"

"Of course they are. They have to."

She left for a second, then returned with an armload of papers of some sort, most of them yellow, which she simply dumped on the floor.

She beamed at them.

"Some are congratulatory telegrams. The rest are applications."

"Applications to come to school here?"

"Yes. All told, we have five thousand new applications, with more pouring in, despite the time of day."

"My God."

"Why are you so surprised? Why should anyone be surprised? I myself am surprised that the number is not higher still. Think about it, from the student's perspective: you can go to another university, pay the tuition you're paying now, plus five or ten thousand dollars extra if you want to study in Paris. Or Vienna. Or Bangkok. Or wherever."

She shook her head.

"Or you can come here and get better teachers, master teachers, teachers who actually love what they're doing, pay half the tuition, and go to Europe or Asia or Africa or Antarctica, for that matter, every summer for absolutely free. Where would *you* want to go to school? Nina, think of this: every university will have to follow this model. The ones that don't will go broke."

She continued:

"All one has to do is take the top off this, just once, and let people see all the money that's being wasted—*their* money, the money they're losing their homes for, the money they've spent their lives scrimping together––let them see it being *wasted* on bureaucrats conferring in Zurich and bookworms writing about extinct shrimp, while their children are getting cheap rooms, eating bad food, and being taught by part-time teachers moonlighting at the local junior college. All one has to do is show them this one time, so that they really *see*."

She shook her head and then said quietly:

"Some of the telegrams reproach me for being *anti-intellectual,* and for hurting the cause of human knowledge, for hindering vital research. Rubbish. The intellect is the mind. *Intellectual* means *using the mind.* Wasting twenty billion dollars of student's and taxpayers' money on people who do nothing constructive—nothing that helps anyone here at the university or anywhere else—is that using the mind? And as for hindering vital research—well, there remain forty nine other such *research institutes* in forty nine other states. If this research is so vital, so cutting edge––let's see how many of those institutions wish to hire our *early retirement faculty.* Indeed, none of them will, which is why the faculty are so outraged in the first place."

A pause.

"It is a far more pernicious sin to force speech from those with nothing to say, than to prohibit it to those with vital thoughts. The latter will frequently speak out, regardless; the former will never shut up."

Silence for a time. Then:

"Are all of those telegrams in support of what you're doing?"

Lucinda Herndon shook her head.

"No. Some are complaints. Some are threats."

"You've gotten threats?"

"Certainly. I've even gotten bomb threats, actually. Threats are the last resort of desperate people. And these are desperate people."

"But the faculty—are they not being supported by professors' groups all over the country?"

"What groups? The American Association of University Professors? The AAUP is debating as we speak whether to put the issue on its calendar in March. March! Nina, the people of whom we're speaking have made careers of mutual disagreement, and mutual isolation. They cannot agree on where the bathroom is. Indeed, they can hardly agree *what* the bathroom is. At what point in the history of this university, or any university, do you remember them acting together bravely and saying: Enough! We stand together!"

Silence for a time. Then:

"Of course, you remember no such time! It should have happened when they saw their classroom podiums being filled by these terribly-compensated and completely unrespected adjunct faculty. They should have stood as one then and said *no*. Teaching here is a revered profession and it will only be done by people adequately paid and professionally treated. They should have done that for the honor of their profession, if not for the realization that they were watching the growth of the very class that was being groomed to destroy them."

She took a sip of wine and shook her head.

"I'm not an ogre," she said, softly. "On Monday— because we're going to have a great many more students and will need teachers—I will offer all of the full-time faculty who have signed up for early retirement, another option. They may stay on here, on with the new faculty. Of course, people such as Arthur Whittington will cheerfully agree, because Arthur's very existence, his very core, is teaching. But they will all work for what everyone else does, and they will bloody well teach ten sections a year. If they don't wish to do this—many will not be able to tolerate it, because many despise teaching—well, they will simply need to find another university to fund this cutting edge research of theirs."

A pause. Then:

"People have for so many years simply tolerated professors, thinking them eccentric and essentially useless, but not harmful. Old Professor Suggs, strolling around the campus, mumbling poetry to himself."

She leaned forward:

"And that remains true to a certain extent for the faculty we now find ourselves supporting. They are indeed useless. But harmless? They are taking our money, and giving us nothing back for it. I don't find that harmless."

Then, breathing deeply, she continued:

"Never doubt that a small group of dedicated people can change the world. Indeed, that's the only thing that ever has."

"Margaret Mead."

"Very good, Nina. And now I must ask. The job I offered you this morning—"

"Yes."

"Have you decided to take it? Will you join my small group of dedicated people?"

"I don't know."

"Is it the work?"

"No. No, I believe in the work. I didn't. I thought at first you were crazy. But now I believe in you. No, it's not the job."

"Is it Rick Barnes?"

"Yes."

"Are you in love with him?"

"No. But I find myself wanting to be where he is."

"Where is he now?"

"He's just walking. And thinking."

"About?"

"The same things I'm thinking about. We're going to meet in half an hour or so at a wine bar on Hacker Street."

"I know it well. It's an Ellerton fixture. Thomas and I used to go there often, alone or with faculty colleagues. You'll like it."

"It's not the bar I'm thinking about."

"But rather?"

"What he's going to ask me."

"And that would be?"

Nina shrugged:

"That's what he's almost certainly thinking about now, while he walks. He's thinking about whether he should ask me to come back with him to his house. Just for a glass of cognac, or something like that. He's wondering if he should invite me; I'm wondering if I should go."

"Nothing wrong with a glass of cognac."

"No, except it wouldn't be for cognac and both of us know that. If I go home with him tonight I'm going to bed with him."

"And you don't know whether you want to do that, and that's bothering you."

"The thing that's bothering me is, I do know whether I *want* to do that. I just don't know whether I *should* do that. And that's a question not even Jane Austen can help me answer."

"Well. I know which answer I'm hoping that you choose, Nina. You and Rick are two of my favorite people. If you stay with him, then you'll be a part of the new Ellerton. And everybody wins."

"I don't know. It's been so long."

"You're still a vibrant woman, Nina. You have a great deal of life in front of you. Savor it. And work with me."

"It's tempting. I have to go now, Lucinda."

"I know you do. Order the house Chardonnay."

Nina rose and walked toward the door.

"There is, of course," she said over her shoulder, "somebody else who's going to have to agree with this."

"Frank?"

She shook her head.
"Furl."
And, so saying, she left the residence.

CHAPTER ELEVEN: THE WINE BAR AND THE WALK

Those knowledgeable with the Ellerton area know there is a wine bar on Hacker Street, which skirts the east side of the campus. Hacker Street is not busy. A few students live there, a few retired professors. But it's tree-lined, with crumbling sidewalks and fallen down fences. There's no traffic to speak of except the occasional bicycle taking a student to class, or ambulance taking a dying ex-professor to the emergency ward, or a dead one to the morgue.

One can go upstairs in the wine bar, sit by a curtained window, listen to the tinkle of piano music wafting up from the lounge downstairs, order a Chardonnay, and—sometimes in January—watch the soft fall of blue-white snow outside, through the trees.

There was no snow now, of course.

But otherwise, everything was exactly as it should have been.

This angered Nina, who'd hoped for a small explosion, a gas leak, a robbery, or something else that might have made ordinary conversation impossible.

But as it happened, nothing.

Drat.

"So, how did the talk with Herndon go?"

"As well as could be expected. She asked me if I wanted the job."

"The job of finding teachers, you mean."

"Yes."

"What did you tell her?"

"That I hadn't made up my mind yet."

Silence for a time.

Rick:

"She must be excited about the night. She's won. She's beaten them all."

"She knows that, but I don't know how excited she seemed. It's as though she had the whole thing planned from the first."

Nina sipped her cold white wine and continued:

"No surprises. She knew what the faculty were going to do—the old, fired, faculty, that is—and what the administrators—bureaucrats, she would call them— were going to do—and what the provost was going to do. Except for the fight he had with you. She didn't plan that."

"Neither did I. I've never liked that guy. We've clashed before on things I've written. We're known enemies. I told him once in public to go to hell, and he shouted back at me that I should—well, it doesn't matter. But when he brought you into the thing—damn, I wish I could have broken his neck."

"Good that you didn't."

"I don't know."

"Anyway, he got what was coming to him. Early retirement."

They both sat for a time, listening to a rising wind in the trees just beyond the upstairs window.

"It's nice here," she said, quietly.

"Yeah. One of my favorite places."

"Did you have a good walk?" she asked.

"I don't remember."

"Where did you go?"

"I don't remember that, either."

"So, had you been drinking?"

"Wish I had. Would be easier now, if I were drunk."

"Well, you could probably just go on drinking Chardonnay."

"You think that might make it easier?"

"Might, you never can tell."

"Do you want to go to bed with me, Rick?"

"Yes."

"All right. Then let's pay the bill and go."

And they did.

The only thing she was later to remember about the walk back to Rick's was how comfortable it was. A thunderstorm had hit, but that did not matter. The low rumblings from scudding clouds, the flashes of lightning illuminating the dark, night sky, the spattering rain, which soaked them as they walked together, her arm around his waist—all of this merely added to the feeling of belonging, of being on the right street at the right time.

"When did you know?" he asked, quietly.

"The first night," she answered.

"Yeah. Me too."

"I tried not to think about it, but every time I tried not to think about it, I realized I was thinking about it. About you. Then yesterday when I saw your house—all I could do was see me in it."

"It's a comfortable house. It's going to get more comfortable now, though."

"I hope so. I hope you won't find me—underfoot."

"That is," he said, squeezing her softly with the palm that was resting on her shoulder, "the last place I expect to find you."

They turned a corner.

The rain eased slightly, but she could hear it splashing in the thick leaves of oak trees which, like she and Rick, seemed to be holding hands above them, their branches intertwined.

"You're talking the job, I assume."

"Yes."

"When will you tell Herndon?"

"Tomorrow, I guess."

"Are you going to want to keep the place you're in now?"

"I don't know."

"You know I want you to come and be with me. And then, after a respectable time, we should—"

She interrupted him.

"Don't worry about that now, Rick. There's your house. Let's just go inside and be together. The other things will work themselves out, in time."

"All right."

"I love this street. These old two-story houses."

"Yep. I spent my childhood climbing the trees in the backyard. I'll show you tomorrow morning."

The climbed the porch, and she could see drops of rain glistening on the hanging swing.

He turned the front door knob.

"I never bother to lock the door," he said. "Hasn't been a crime on this street in—I don't know, a decade, I guess."

He pushed the door open.

She walked in, and he followed, turning on the light switch as he entered.

She looked across the room.

Prone on the sofa, wrapped in a blood-drenched blanket, was the body of the provost.

He had been enfolded like a mummy; his eyes were wide and staring at the ceiling; his beard was drenched with bright red blood.

CHAPTER TWELVE: BEDLAM

Nina left her own body and watched it take three steps into the house. Something in her continued to be a spectator as her hand rose slowly to her mouth, palm pressing now against her front teeth.

From the distance—but closer now, and closer still—they could hear sirens approaching.

Finally, after what could only have been a few seconds, she returned to herself again, once more inhabiting the body of Nina Bannister, which was turning in a slow circle to face windows.

Bright blue lights were everywhere outside now.

"Open the door please! Open the door please!"

The police were banging on the top pane of the door.

"Open it now! Open it right now!"

She looked at Rick, who had moved in the direction of the couch and was staring down at the body.

"Rick?"

He merely shook his head as the shouting outside continued:

Finally, he said:

"You have to open the door."

"Rick, is it the provost?"

"Yes."

"He's dead?"

"Shot in the chest. Open the door, Nina."

Taking two steps forward, she did so.

A man entered first; then a woman.

She was more aware of the uniforms than of the faces.

"Oh, God," she heard dimly behind her, from one of the officers.

Then static and scrabble of microphone voices.

"We need help! We need backup! Yes! Yes, now! No, I have the perpetrators. No, send—"

And a woman—a big woman, a forceful but gentle woman, huge arms around her, leading her—

"We have to go, ma'am. You have to come with us."

More lights. Lights everywhere. A thousand coyotes all moaning, howling—the whole world was sirens and blue lights, and Rick's house was under water now—people, uniformed people, making their way here and there, running into the furniture.

Why were they running into the furniture?

Make them stop!

It's time to wake up, she told herself. *Why can't I wake up from this dream?*

Wake up! Wake up, dammit!

But the woman, always pulling on her...

"Come on, honey. You have to come with us. It'll be all right."

But from nearer the sofa, she kept hearing voices, first one, then the other, then a man, then a woman:

"His chest is blown open."

And the woman, leading her.

"It's going to be all right. You just have to come with us. I'll take care of you, honey. I won't let anything happen to you."

Finally, being led outside and through the doorway, she said:

"Rick?"

"All right, dear. He's coming too."

"Where is Rick? I want Rick!"

"They're bringing him in another car. He's coming along."

"I want to be with him!"

"You will."

"What happened? What happened?"

"We don't know yet. We're going to find out."

"But that man is dead! He's dead back there!"

"Just be careful now, dear. Bend your head down. What's your name, dear?"

"Nina! I'm Nina!"

"That's right, Nina. Real good. Real good, girl! You're almost in now."

"We were—just walking, and we went inside and—"

"I understand. Now—let's get you belted in—"

An ambulance…two ambulances—my God that's a helicopter—there's flashing, and flashing, and flashing—

"Let's go! Let's go! Let's go!"

The car, moving away now.

"I have to put these handcuffs on you. Hold out your arms."

"No, I—"

"It will only be for a while, dear. We'll take them off real soon."

"Oh, God—they're cold! I can't—I can't move my hands!"

"It's all right!"

"I can't move!"

"Be still, honey!"

More hands—how many people are in the back here with me?

I can't move!

"Rick! Rick!"

"You'll be back with him real soon!"

The car moved toward downtown, as microphones on squad cars around the city broadcast the report that the provost of Ellerton University had been shot to death in the home of the reporter he had, only hours earlier, fought with.

That reporter, along with an unidentified woman, were being taken into custody.

CHAPTER THIRTEEN: A WORLD DEVOID OF SENSE

The main city police office was located almost directly opposite a completely impersonal Chase Bank building, and within a four-block radius of at least a dozen restaurants and bars.

Usually at ten in the evening, it was almost deserted.

Now, though, it had begun to draw media vehicles with an almost magnetic power.

Everyone in the city was in the process of hearing about the ghastly murder that had taken place in an environment completely alien to violence of any kind.

So that Nina, taken from the squad car in handcuffs, was forced to walk through a growing knot of reporters, officers, gawkers, more officers, university officials, and newly-awakened street people.

She'd never been in handcuffs before.

"Just come right through here, miss."

"All right."

Three people—the original policewoman who'd herded her into the car, and two other officers—both men—surrounded her as she entered the building.

"Just right through here. It's going to be all right."

"Listen…"

"We won't let anything happen to you."

"Where is Rick? Where did you take him?"

"He's coming, ma'am."

"Can I talk to him?"

The woman officer looked quickly at both men, who shook their heads in tandem.

"No, ma'am."

"I just need to see him! Just see him!"

"Come with me, ma'am."

"Where are we going?"

"Into the bathroom. I have to check you."

"For what?"

"Just come with me."

"What are you checking me for?"

"You're on suicide watch. We have to see that you don't have any sharp objects."

"I'm not about to commit suicide!"

"I know that, dear. It's just procedure. Come on. Once I check you out, I can take off these cuffs."

"I—"

"Come on, please. This won't take long."

Reluctantly, she allowed herself to be led by the woman into a bathroom of sorts.

The walls were padded.

Oh, God, she thought.

"All right, here we go."

"You're taking those off?"

"Yes, ma'am. If you promise me you won't do anything to make me put them back on you."

"I promise."

'You're okay now?"

"I'm okay. I didn't kill anybody!"

"That's all right. Let's just do one thing at a time. Now. Let's get these handcuffs off you."

"Oh, thank you. Thank God."

"That's all right, baby. Now take your blouse off."

Nina did so, then allowed herself to be quickly searched.

"You don't seem to have anything on you."

"No. I don't."

"Okay, then wait."

The woman went to the door of the bathroom, opened it, said a few words quietly, then came back.

"You want to sit over there on that bench? Right by the corner."

"All right."

Nina did so.

The woman pulled up a rotating stool, and sat facing her, then produced a cell phone.

"Here. You may make one call. Most people elect to call their lawyer."

"Thank you! Oh, God, thank you!"

Nina grabbed the phone with one hand and, with the other, dialed a number she knew by heart.

Pause.

Buzz. Buzz.

Then:

"Jackson Bennett here."

She was almost crying:

"Jackson—"

"What is it, Nina? Are you at Ellerton?"

"Jackson, I'm in jail. They think—"

"Just don't talk, Nina. I'll be up there as soon as I can."

And he hung up.

The woman opposite her took the cell phone back.

Outside, she could tell there was pandemonium.

More sirens, people pouring into the central office.

She found herself led down a corridor, past one room, past another. She thought of clinics, of doctors' waiting rooms.

"Just—right in here."

"What about Rick? You said I could see Rick!"

The woman who'd offered her the phone was gone now. Nina was surrounded by people, a professional-looking woman, two uniformed officers, and one man in a business suit.

One of the officers spoke to her:

"Right in here. We've got to ask you some questions. Can you answer questions?"

"Yes. I'm all right."

"Good. First, you have to tell us: have you taken anything?"

"What?"

"Have you taken anything?"

"You mean drugs?"

"Yes, ma'am."

"No, for God's sake!"

"Do you feel that you're in control of your actions?"

"Yes!"

The woman knelt, put her hands on Nina's knees, and said quietly:

"I'm Doctor Joan Robertson. I'm a police psychiatrist. You have to know that you can talk to me, all right?"

"Yes!"

"You understand? I'm not here to hurt you; no one wants to hurt you."

"I don't understand what's happened!"

"That's what *we* want. We want to understand, Nina."

"Do you think we killed that man? Rick and I?"

"Just try to answer my questions: can you do that?"

"Yes!"

"Do you understand where you are?"

"Yes!"

"Where are you?"

"I'm in jail!"

"Okay. Now. What's your name?"

"Nina Bannister."

"What do you do, Nina?"

"I'm a teacher. I'm here at Ellerton to teach an English course."

"You're on the regular faculty?"

"No, it's a special prize I won. I'm just here for a semester."

"All right. Now: have you taken any kind of a controlled substance, Nina?"

"No! I've already told them that!"

"All right. We're just going to have a doctor look at you now."

"Why?"

"He's just going to look at your eyes and take your blood pressure."

"My eyes are fine! Although I have to tell you, my blood pressure might be a little elevated right now, because I'm being accused of murder!"

Was that a laugh? Did someone in the back of the room actually laugh?

Then she began to be prodded and rapped and gazed at by a doctor, by a nurse—

"She's okay."

"No drugs?"

"No. She's right. Blood pressure's elevated, but she's clean."

"We can talk to her?"

"Looks like it."

"All right, Nina. You seem to know where you are. You seem to be rational. Do you think you can talk about this?"

"Yes!"

"All right," said the woman who'd introduced herself as Joan Robinson.

Then:

"Nina—"

She gestured at a silver-haired man who was wearing what seemed like a business suit.

"This is Roger Thompson. He's a police inspector. He's going to ask you some questions."

"All right."

Thompson sat down.

The two of them were sitting in straight chairs, facing each other.

"Nina, just try to tell us what happened."

"Nothing happened!"

"Stay calm."

"That's a little difficult to do!"

"I understand, just back up, and try to tell us what happened."

"Nothing happened! Rick and I were just—"

"You mean Mr. Barnes?"

"Yes!"

"What about him?"

"We were in the wine bar—and then we—"

"You had been drinking?"

"Just a glass of wine."

"Only one glass!"

"Yes, that's what I just told you! And then we walked together back to his house."

"You're having a relationship with Mr. Barnes?"

"No!"

"Really? Why were you going back to his house?"

"I—we were—it's complicated."

"All right. Then go on."

"There's nothing to go on to! Rick opened the door, and we just walked in. When we got inside we saw the provost, lying on the couch. His body was wrapped in a blanket. Rick walked toward him, looked at him, and told me he was dead."

"Do you know how he died, Nina?"

"Rick said he'd been shot in the chest."

"Do you know who shot him?"

"No, that's what I've been telling you!"

"Did one of you shoot him?"

"No, no, we just came home and found him there!"

"Do you know how he got into Mr. Barnes' house?"

"Of course I don't know."

"He was just there?"

"Yes!"

"Wrapped in a blanket, lying dead on the couch."

"That's what I've been telling you!"

"Do you remember, earlier in the evening, at the stadium?"

"Of course, I remember it!"

"Mr. Barnes attacked the provost."

"Okay, he attacked him!"

"After the provost mentioned you, and called you Mr. Barnes' girlfriend?"

"Yes, that happened! But nothing else!"

"Nothing afterward?"

"No, that's what I've been telling you!"

"What did happen afterward?"

"After what?"

"After President Herndon's speech at the stadium. Did the two of you stay to hear that speech?"

"Yes, we had to! Rick was writing a story about it!"

"Did anyone see you there?"

"I don't know! What difference does it make?"

"It makes a great deal of difference, Ms. Bannister. We have to try to re-create the events of the evening, after the provost left the stadium. Now: do you remember precisely what you yourself did?"

"Of course. I got a note saying that I was invited to the president's house."

"A note?"

"Yes."

"Who delivered it?"

"A boy, an undergraduate."

"What was his name?"

"I don't know!"

"You received a note from a boy you didn't know, saying you were to come to the president's house."

"Yes!"

"For what purpose?"

"Oysters."

"Oysters?"

"Yes. We were going to have a late supper of oysters."

"And did you go?"

"Yes!"

"How did you get there?"

"I walked!"

"With Mr. Barnes?"

"No."

"What then did Mr. Barnes do?"

"He—he needed some time alone."

"Was he invited to the president's house?"

"Well, actually the note just mentioned me."

"And do you have that note still?"

"No, I threw it away!"

"Why did you do that?"

"Why *wouldn't* I do that? It was just a hand-scrawled note!"

"The president invited you to her house at ten o'clock, after she'd just given one of the biggest speeches of her life—by means of a hand-scrawled note? Doesn't that seem peculiar?"

"*Everything* that's happened since 8:30 this morning—oh my lord, this has all happened in fourteen hours, in this one town, this one campus; it's like a Greek tragedy!"

"All right. So then, according to your story, you walked to the president's house. Did you go in immediately?"

"No."

"What did you do?"

"It was a nice night. I just sat on the swing and waited."

"You didn't talk to anyone?"

"No, the place was deserted. I assumed that all of the security people were at the stadium, guarding Lucinda. While I sat on the swing, I heard some cars arrive at the main entrance."

"And finally?"

"At almost exactly nine o'clock, Lucinda opened the door."

"Then you went in, and had your meal."

"Yes."

"Alone."

"Yes."

"No one served you?"

"No, Lucinda said she had dismissed the staff for the night. Everything was ready for us."

"How long were you with President Herndon?"

"I don't know. We sat by the fire and had cognac, then went into the kitchen and ate oysters. We had a nice time. I guess it took an hour."

"Then you left."

"Yes."

"And did what?"

"Like I said earlier. I walked to the wine bar."

"Which one?"

"I think it was on Hacker Street."

"And there you had drinks with Mr. Barnes."

"A drink. We had one drink a piece."

"What did you talk about?"

"I don't remember," Nina lied (because she did remember).

But it was none of these people's business.

"What did Mr. Barnes talk about?"

"It's like I say, I don't remember."

"Did he tell you what he'd been doing between the time you left him at the stadium and you met him at the wine bar?"

"No."

"He said nothing at all about that period of time?"

"Well, he…"

"Well, he what?"

"He said he'd been walking."

"Walking where?"

She paused, knowing how her answer was going to sound.

Then she answered, anyway, because there was nothing else she could do.

"He said he couldn't remember."

"He couldn't remember?"

"No."

"Had he been drinking? Before the wine bar, I mean?"

"No."

"You're sure?"

"Yes."

"How?"

"I would know if he'd been drinking."

"So what you're telling me is, you ate with the president, just the two of you. Then, around ten o'clock, you walked to a wine bar on Hacker Street, where you met Mr. Barnes. Mr. Barnes had attacked the provost earlier in the evening, because the provost had made a reference to you, Mr. Barnes' girlfriend. You can be seen on camera embracing Mr. Barnes."

"I was just trying to hold him back."

"You can be seen on camera holding Mr. Barnes' hand, even before the altercation had begun. Were you holding him back then?"

"No."

"What were you doing?"

"Holding hands. People hold hands sometime."

"But you were not having a romantic relationship with him?"

"No."

"And during the time you had a glass of wine together at the wine bar, he could not remember where he'd been, or what he'd been doing, the hour and a half before the two of you met."

"That's right."

"Didn't that strike you as odd?"

"Well, he had a good many things on his mind. He was thinking about…"

"About luring the provost to his house under some pretense, and shooting him?"

"No, that's not what he was thinking about."

"How do you know?"

"Because he was thinking about—"

Going to bed with me going to bed with me going to bed with me—

"He was thinking about—"

"What? What, Ms. Bannister?"

"He was thinking about—"

The door to the room burst open and another officer burst in, saying:

"Ms. Bannister's attorney is here."

And Adam Marsh walked through the door.

CHAPTER FOURTEEN: MEMORIES OF PERRY MASON

She remembered the full white beard, the athletic build, and even the pronounced limp. But she had not remembered the sparkle in his blue eyes as he looked at her, and that turned colder as he addressed the others in the room.

"Have you attempted an interrogation of my client without my being there?"

Thompson:

"We didn't know she was your client."

"Well, whatever she said is not going to be admissible in any court, I hope you know that."

Thompson merely nodded and said, curtly:

"She hasn't said all that much, if you want to know the truth."

"Maybe because she doesn't know all that much."

"She knows something, and we need to hear it."

"She needs to go home. She's had a shock."

"At least she's alive. That's more than anyone can say for the provost. And as for her going anywhere, I'd forget that."

"Is she under arrest?"

"She will be as soon as she tries to leave the building, with or without a lawyer. For God's sakes, Marsh, a man was murdered not less than two hours ago. The body was found in Rick Barnes' house. The victim had been attacked by Barnes—clearly with this woman urging Barnes on—on national television. Arriving officers found these two standing in the middle of the room, staring down at the body. And you want to do what? Walk out and take her to the nearest Holiday Inn?"

Adam Marsh stepped forward and said, more softly now:

"She's a schoolteacher, not a Mafia hit man."

"I appreciate her profession; I'm sure she's done a lot of good in her life."

"Let me just take her to her house, where she can spend the night. I'll vouch for her. You can even surround the place with cops."

"She's already in a place that's surrounded by cops, and that's where she's going to stay. Think about it, do you really want to take her out of here? Why, man, the whole town is crawling with news media! There were a thousand here just to report on Herndon's *revolution*, or whatever she's calling it. Now the second most important official at the university gets his chest blown open with a twenty-gauge shotgun. You think you're going to be able to drive her away from here and not be noticed? The provost's wife, Amy? She's grief-stricken and may have to be hospitalized. She's shouting that Ms. Bannister and Mr. Barnes should be hanged immediately. And that she wants to tear both of them to pieces! Your client ought to be thankful we're not turning her over to the press."

Adam Marsh was silent for a time; then he said:

"All right. At least let me talk with her. Alone."

"That's your right. Are you sure she's really your client?"

Marsh looked at her:

"Nina, do you want me for a lawyer?"

"Of course I do! Jackson Bennett is coming, but I don't know when he's going to get here."

"Jackson's a good man; I know him. But for right now—" He then looked back at the circle of people surrounding them:

"I'm her lawyer."

"All right. Take her down the hall, the officers will show you to a room."

"It would be nice if the officers could show us a couple of cups of coffee too."

"Okay, but don't push your luck. You've got her for half an hour. Then she has to be processed."

That sounded ominous to Nina, but she tried to block it from her mind and think of only Marsh's kind face, and the prospect of coffee.

Within a matter of some minutes, she was looking at the one and sipping the other.

They had been taken to a room that, if not exactly comfortable, was at least better than the way she imagined Auschwitz. It had on the wall the kind of pictures that could be purchased in supermarkets, and it was at least as cozy and welcoming as a doctor's waiting room.

The coffee was wretched, but there was Splenda to mask the taste.

"How are you holding up to this ordeal, Nina?"

She shrugged:

"Not very well. I keep expecting to break out in tears. I'm not sure why that hasn't happened already."

"It hasn't happened because you're tough. I've just been talking to Rick about some of the things you've been through."

"Funny. I've been through a lot in the last year or so, but this is the first time I've been arrested for murder."

Marsh shrugged.

"A retired high school English teacher living in a little Mississippi town. It had to happen eventually."

"I guess. Adam, where is Rick?"

"Down the hall."

"Being questioned?"

A shake of the head:

"No, Rick called me immediately, even before he got here. I was able to stop them from interrogating him. Sorry I was too late in your case."

"Is he okay?"

"He's like you, as well as can be expected."

"I'd like to see him."

"They're not going to allow that, Nina."

"Why not?"

He paused for a time, then breathed deeply and said:

"Nina, they think the two of you killed this man."

"I know that, but—"

"They want to keep you separated so that you can't agree on your story."

"Our alibi."

"If you want to call it that. But you've got to believe me: Rick's all right."

The air conditioner came on, went off, came on.

She, possibly coming out of a state of shock, started remembering things.

The way the wine had tasted; the way Rick's eyes looked; the way it felt, the two of them, walking back from the wine bar—

—the body of the provost, staring up at her.

And all the things that had happened since then.

It was Adam Marsh's voice that called her back to reality.

"After we finish here, Nina, they're going to process you."

"I know. I heard."

"That means they will fingerprint you. Have you ever been fingerprinted?"

"No, but I've seen it done on TV. I think I'll be able to manage."

"They'll keep you here overnight. I think I can manage to get you away from the general population. It will be a spare room, but you'll be alone."

"Well," she said, "heaven for comfort, hell for society."

"That's one way to look at it."

Silence for a time, then from Marsh:

"I was able to talk with Rick. I don't want to belabor all this now and burden you with details. Just let me be sure I've got this right: the two of you heard Herndon's speech at the stadium. After that, Rick went walking, and you went to have a late dinner with the president. You met around ten o'clock at the wine bar. You each had one glass of wine, then walked together to his place. When you went inside, you found the provost's body."

"Yes, that's all true."

The door opened and a young policewoman stepped in.

"Mr. Marsh?"

"We have," said Marsh, "at least another fifteen minutes."

"No, that's not it, sir. It's just that Officer Thompson wanted me to give you this."

She handed Marsh a sheet of paper and then left.

Marsh regarded the paper for a time.

"What is it?" asked Nina.

"Report."

"Stating?"

He shook his head.

"We'll go into it in a minute. But for now, Nina, I've got to ask you something. You can tell me the absolute truth, or you can just tell me to go to hell. But I've got to remind you, that there are two people it's deadly to lie to: your doctor and your lawyer."

"Did you learn that in law school?"

"No, I saw it on *Perry Mason*."

"Well, it's good that you still have a sense of humor, Mr. Marsh."

"I'm not trying to be funny. And it's Adam."

"All right, Adam. I understand what you're saying. Ask away."

"Were you and Rick—"

"We were going back to his place to go to bed together."

He looked down at the carpet as though embarrassed, then asked:

"You hadn't gone to bed together before?"

"No."

"You had not been lovers?"

"No. Am I going to have to go into this?"

"I don't know. But you were seen holding hands together, you had a glass of wine together, you walked around ten o'clock back to his place—if you deny at least some romantic interest, the prosecution is going to make you look like liars, and they're going on to say that you must think the public consists of a bunch of imbeciles."

"I understand."

"So you'll have to make that decision."

"All right. But now, Mr.—Adam, I have to ask some questions of my own."

"Go ahead."

"The story Rick and I told you is true. Down to the smallest detail. I didn't add the part about my own personal feelings a few minutes ago with Officer Thompson because—well, I didn't think that was any of his business."

"Okay."

"But now my question to you is: how did this happen? We were in Rick's house earlier in the afternoon, about, say, nine o'clock. But not since then.

And the provost was at the stadium at seven o'clock. At ten, he was lying dead on Rick's sofa. What happened? How did he get there? Who shot him? And with what?"

Marsh simply shook his head and said:

"I don't know how he came to be there, Nina. I don't know who shot him. But I do know one thing, because it's here in the report I just was handed."

"What?"

"I know what he was shot with. He was shot with the twenty gauge shotgun that Rick and I always took with us when we went out to our cabin to shoot doves."

She sat for a time, stunned.

The air conditioner went on and off.

The next half hour was somewhat unreal. It was as though she were being tested for her driver's license, given the number of questions asked and forms filled out. Adam Marsh came and went, pleading, always unsuccessfully, to have her released.

These attempts culminated at precisely eleven thirty—she could remember glancing up at a circular clock above the door of whatever room she was in— when Penn Robinson walked in.

He crossed the room hurriedly and embraced her. She took some comfort in the muscular upper body that was almost breaking her ribs.

"Nina, I'm so sorry for all this. I just found out what happened a little over an hour ago. I've been with Rick."

"Is he all right?"

"He's fine. He's a tough guy. His main worry is about you."

"I'll survive."

"We're trying to get you out, so that you don't have to sleep here tonight."

"I know."

"Rick told me the story. I'm writing it up myself. Clearly neither one of you has the slightest idea of how the man was shot, or who did it."

"No, we don't. It just doesn't make sense."

"The main thing is that—"

Roger Thompson entered the room then and walked straight to Nina. Looking down at her, he said:

"Ms. Bannister?"

"Yes?"

"We need to take you into fingerprinting now."

She breathed deeply:

"All right. If it has to be done—"

"It has to be done. Then we have to get something for you to wear."

Robinson:

"Roger, surely you can't be serious about keeping her here."

"Of course, I'm serious. She's our prime murder suspect."

"Look, what if I vouch for her!"

"I don't care who vouches for her. There is no way the woman leaves this building. If I let her do so, the district attorney would have my hide."

"*The Gazette* will be happy to post bond."

"If there is bond. We'll let a judge decide that tomorrow."

"But Roger, think! Does this look like a woman who pointed a twenty-gauge shotgun at a man and pulled the trigger?"

"No, it looks like the girlfriend of a man who did that."

"If I and Adam Marsh—"

"You and Adam Marsh can both go home."

"Is there no way at all that—"

"There is no way at all, now stop wasting my time!"

"There is no person who can help here?"

"I'm telling you, there's no one. No please let me do my job!"

The door burst open at that point, and Peter Stockton entered.

He glared for an instant at everyone in the room.

Then he took a cell phone from his pants pocket, popped it open, and shouted into it:

"All right, he's here. Talk to him."

He handed the phone to Roger Thompson, who put it to his ear and said:

"This is Roger Thompson."

Then silence, except for a few nods.

Finally, Thompson clamped the phone shut and handed it back to Peter Stockton, who said, softly, to Nina:

"Let's go, Ms. Bannister."

Together, with no one making a move to stop them, they left the building.

CHAPTER FIFTEEN: SANCTUARY

A limousine, black and shiny and absurdly long, was waiting for them in a back alley.

"Residence," Stockton growled to the driver, who pulled slowly around the building and out into traffic.

Nina settled back into the leather seat, said "Thank God," to God, and "Who was on the cell phone?" to Peter Stockton.

God answered by allowing her to stay in the limousine which was taking her away from jail; Peter Stockton answered by saying:

"District Attorney."

"You know him?"

"I made him. Without me, he'd still be dog catcher. And not very good at that damned job either. They're all a bunch of idiots. Keep a lady like you in a jail overnight."

"Mr. Stockton—"

"Pete."

"Pete, how did you learn about this mess?"

"Hell, everybody knows about it. I heard on the evening news. Then I called Lucinda. I knew I could get you out, but I wasn't too sure what I was going to do with you. Wouldn't look too good, you staying at my place. She said what I hoped she would, that I could bring you over to the residence. You'll get a good night's sleep there; she and I will see to that."

The twin hums of motor and air conditioner serenaded each other as the car snaked its way back through campus.

"We didn't kill that man, Pete."

"That's too bad," he growled.

"Pardon?"

"Somebody killed him. Blew his chest open. If I can find out who did it, I'll give the guy or gal a million dollars."

"You didn't like him?"

"Nobody liked him. And he made Lucinda's life a living hell. Every dollar she brought into the university, and that she had visions for, he blocked. More of those damned articles and more of those damned bureaucrats. Plus the man was a skunk. Are you sure the two of you didn't kill him?"

"Pretty sure. I think I'd remember."

"Damn. Have to keep my money where it is."

They could see the residence now, glowing in front of them.

"What's going to happen next?"

"As far as I can tell," he said, "there'll be a formal hearing tomorrow at nine o'clock. Judge and all. You two will get to tell your stories. The first thing is, though, you need a good night's sleep."

"I'm not too sure how easy that's going to be."

"Easier here, I imagine, than back in the jail."

"That's very true, Pete. And thank you. Thank you for getting me out."

"Was my pleasure, ma'am. Sorry I couldn't do the same for Barnes. But even with all the pull I had, even with my promising to get that D.A. fired if he didn't go along with me—even with all that, there was no way they were going to let you two see each other."

"I understand."

"I like Barnes. I like the way he writes. Clear, doesn't make up words or beat around the bush. I even like his newspaper except it's—"

"I know. Too liberal."

"You think so too, huh?"

"What else could one think?"

"Well, anyway, here we are. And there's Lucinda!"

She was waiting for them, wearing a dark blue robe, and standing on the veranda.

How many years had passed, Nina found herself wondering, *since eight thirty this morning when the two of them had walked from this space, across the campus, into the faculty meeting?*

Ten years? A hundred years?

"Nina!"

The two of them embraced.

Then cried.

Finally, Lucinda:

"It's all right, Nina. It will all be all right, now. And thank you, Peter. You're always there for me. Always."

"We got her out. That's the main thing."

"Now, come inside, Nina. We'll put you in a quiet, interior room. You won't hear a thing all night. And here, over here on this little table, there's a glass of milk for you."

"Thank you."

Nina picked it up, drank from it, and drank again.

"You're going to need a good night's sleep."

"I'm not sure I'll be able to sleep."

"Of course, you will. You'll sleep like a log. Tomorrow we shall all eat breakfast together, like civilized people. I've invited Mr. Marsh over—I'm told he is attorney for both you and Richard."

"That's true."

"Then tomorrow, at nine, we shall all talk before the judge. I'll tell him what a splendid teacher you are, and what a credit to the community."

"Thank you, Lucinda."

"It will be my great pleasure."

They were moving inside now, and Nina
remembered the room with the fireplace, where the two
of them had drunk sherry.

"I'll have to excuse myself now, ladies. If there's
anything more I can do—"

Lucinda:

"Could you take the two of us downtown tomorrow?
I think we both would feel more comfortable riding
with you."

"Of course, I could. I'll have my car come around
about eight thirty. We'll all go together."

"Wonderful."

"Good night then."

So saying, he bowed and left.

Nina followed Lucinda down a long corridor, which,
strangely, was beginning to swim before her eyes.

"I'm getting really tired," she said.

"Of course you are. Just follow me. I've had the bed
made, and a nightgown laid out for you to sleep in."

"Thank you."

"It's nothing."

"And Lucinda, you're telling the judge about my
teaching will be kind of you. There's something else
that's probably going to be more important, though."

"And that will be?"

"Talk about the oysters."

"The what, dear?"

"Our oyster meal. If I was here eating with you—"

"Oh, of course. That goes without saying. Now
come, in here."

She opened the door to an elegantly furnished
bedroom.

"I wish I had a book," said Nina, making her way to
the bed and picking up a nightgown that Lucinda had
laid out for her.

"You won't need one, I promise."

"It's always hard for me to sleep without reading. And given everything that's happened today—"

"You'll go right to sleep."

"I do feel kind of groggy."

"Of course, you do."

"Maybe it's just that I'm exhausted."

"That's possible, Nina. Or it may be the sleeping tablet I put in your milk. Now good night, and I'll see you in the morning."

Within five minutes, Nina was asleep.

The following morning, when she awoke, she was unable even to remember putting on the nightgown.

CHAPTER SIXTEEN: THE HEARING

She was not surprised that she slept soundly, given the medication she'd taken, but rather that she felt so refreshed at 7:30 the following morning. No headache, no drowsiness, no feelings of disorientation or dizziness—just a complete sense of freshness, as though she were back home with Furl and her Vespa, getting ready to walk on the beach and go to Bagatelli's for croissants.

"That was some sleeping pill you gave me," she announced to Lucinda Herndon, upon entering the breakfast room.

"Yes, Thomas discovered it some years ago. He suffered so from the tension connected with the job. I knew it would make you sleep. I hope there are no side effects."

"No, I feel great. Good morning, Adam."

Adam Marsh stood, sipped a cup of coffee, and smiled.

"Good morning, yourself."

The room was small, but, like everything else in the residence, elegantly appointed. A silver coffee service gleamed on the table, and plates of bacon and eggs soon appeared before them as if by magic.

"Adam," said Lucinda Herndon, "was kind enough to come by. I thought it might be best if we could talk before the hearing."

"Good idea," Nina replied, buttering a roll. "Adam, have you heard from Rick?"

"Yes. I just came from the jail. He slept okay. Obviously, he's not exactly on top of the world right now."

"Have you been able to learn anything since last night?"

"A few things. The autopsy report came in a little over an hour ago. They think the provost was shot about nine thirty, about an hour before you two found the body."

"At nine thirty, I was here, having a late dinner with Lucinda., so that clears me. The problem is Rick. He's got to try to remember where he walked. There's a chance someone saw him. But as it is, he's got no alibi at all. And there are so many other things that don't make sense. What was the provost doing at Rick's house in the first place?"

"I don't know, Nina."

They ate in silence for a time, while the events of the previous day began replaying themselves in Nina's mind.

"What's the situation with the university?" she asked.

"Well, President Herndon's speech last night was certainly a coup," said Marsh. "The provost thought he had marshalled enough support to remove her and install himself as president. He'd already lined up a team of psychologists to testify that she was entering dementia, and another team of lawyers to label the contracts and the early retirement papers invalid."

Lucinda Herndon merely smiled:

"I'm sorry I could not have been at the stadium to see his face. His and Barbara's."

"There was very little either of them could do. Tuition cut in half. That alone made you the most popular president in the history of education. That, and, word is already going around the state and the country that anyone who goes to school here and wants to, gets a free study tour in Europe, or God knows where else."

"So the battle is over?" asked Nina. "The old faculty and administration are really gone?"

Marsh shrugged:

"It's not that easy," he said. "Some of them, realizing they won't have to work for the rest of their lives, are really pretty happy about it. They can go and live the rest of their lives in Paris if they want. Others are fighting it, of course. But Rick's stories were very effective. Lucinda started a true national revolution. Parents, political leaders, students themselves—people all over are looking closely at universities and asking hard questions."

"Like?"

"Like what *is* this *research* that you're spending so much money on? It's one thing to figure out how to cure cancer; it's a whole different thing to use tax money finding out about extinct shrimp. And the same people are asking themselves, does any university really need *three* assistant coordinators of planning and development? What in heaven's name do these people do, anyway?"

"Lucy," Nina said, looking at the president, "you should be very proud."

But Lucinda Herndon merely shook her head:

"I would be, of course. I just did what needed doing, and what no one else seemed to have the stomach for. True university reform has never taken place in my life time, and, as the monstrous amoeba that is the research university grew and swelled, it became such a daunting creature that no one dared attack it."

"And you did."

"Yes, but that's not the attack that worries me right now. The provost may not have been one of my favorite people, but he did not deserve what happened to him.

Nor did Rick and you deserve what you were put through last night."

"It seems like a dream. Or rather a nightmare. Walking through that door, seeing the couch, all the blood—"

"Adam," asked the president, "what about the murder weapon?"

"The shotgun? It's Rick's all right. He kept it hanging on the wall above the couch. I've been over to his place several times, and it's always been there. That is, when he's not dove hunting."

"No, that's not what I'm talking about. I was referring to finger prints. I'm an administrator not a detective; but one hears about, reads about police procedure…"

Adam Marsh shook his head.

"No prints. Whoever shot the provost was smart. The gun had been wiped clean."

Silence for a time.

Then Nina:

"What will happen this morning at nine o'clock?"

Marsh set down his coffee cup and shrugged.

"It's a standard preliminary hearing, before a judge. The district attorney will make the case that Rick and Nina are the only suspects, and that the case against them is so damning that they must be held, without bail, for trial. I'll tell their side of the story. I'll also ask you to testify briefly, President Herndon, if I've understood things correctly, Nina was here with you from nine to almost ten."

Lucinda Herndon hesitated for a time, then said:

"Yes. Of course, I'll be happy to testify to that."

"It might be good if you'd talk a little about Nina herself. How you came to know her. Your opinion of her as a teacher. Why you brought her here to take part in this Golden Age Teacher Award program."

"I understand."

"And as for Rick, he's got a whole town full of character witnesses. Everybody knows him and likes him. The problem is, everybody also knows he's had a personal feud with the provost for years. And that attack last night didn't help things."

"I think," said Nina, quietly, "that he was just sticking up for my honor."

"Maybe, but the provost had just sued his paper and threatened his job. Rick's been a reporter in this town for his whole life. The district attorney is going to make the point that people have killed for less compelling reasons than those. And then there's…"

He hesitated.

"What?" Nina asked.

"The thing we talked about last night. The D.A. is almost certainly going to want to know about your relationship with Rick."

"Adam," said Lucinda Herndon, "surely that's a personal matter between Nina and Richard."

Marsh shook his head.

"It *was* personal before last night. But now everything's on the table."

Nina was about to speak, to repeat what she'd said the evening before.

She was about to say 'We were about to go to bed together.'

But a horrible thought came into her mind.

What if Rick *had* murdered the provost?

He had attacked the man only a little more than an hour earlier. There had been a kind of rage in his eyes. And the story of walking, but not knowing where he was going? It made no sense. The man had been murdered with Rick's shotgun, and found in Rick's house.

After having threatened Rick's job.

His career, actually.

His life.

What if he *had* done it?

What did she really know of this man?

Enough to decide to go to bed with him.

How stupid she was.

A woman in her late sixties, a respected woman—acting like a schoolgirl.

How stupid she was.

And what if he, this man she barely knew, really did take a shotgun and blow open the provost's chest?

That was absurd, absolutely absurd.

But it could have happened.

She thought for a time more.

No. It could not have happened. Even if she'd been wrong, completely wrong about this man she had come to feel so comfortable around—even if she could have been stupid enough to misjudge a human being so completely—it still made no sense.

Why would he have returned to the house with her?

Rick would have tried to dispose of the body somehow.

He would not have led Nina straight to it.

No, it made no sense.

But nothing else did either.

She was thinking these thoughts when Peter Stockton drove up in a chauffeured limousine.

It was time to go to court.

CHAPTER SEVENTEEN: BEFORE THE LAW

It was all very much like a television show or a black and white movie.

The judge, stern looking, seated high above the rest of them. The District Attorney, silver-haired, black-rimmed glasses. Marsh, comforting, seated beside her and smiling as often as possible. Rick, dressed in a business suit, at a table next to her and Marsh, scuffling his shoes nervously on the tile floor of the courtroom.

A crowd outside, but no reporters allowed to hear or tape the proceedings.

Somehow she was not that worried about herself. The dinner at the residence would save her. When the provost had been murdered, she had been sipping sherry and eating oysters.

But Rick?

Someone had set him up. But who, and how?

"All right," said the judge, "let's begin. Mr. District Attorney, what case does the state intend to make?"

The man standing some feet away from her could have been an insurance agent. And, when she thought about it, she realized that he was, in fact, a salesman of sorts. He was selling a version of reality that would make her, Nina, as much a murderer as one of the people she'd caught in recent months.

"The state, your honor, will prove that the co-defendants, Ms. Nina Bannister and Mr. Richard Barnes, did willfully do murder on Dr. Charles Iverson, who was shot last night some time between the hours of eight and ten o'clock. The shooting took place at the home of Mr. Barnes and was performed with a weapon belonging to, and registered to, same Mr. Barnes. The state will further show that Mr. Barnes and Dr. Iverson had bitter feelings toward each other, feelings stemming often from Mr. Barnes' reporting of certain events that transpired over a lengthy time frame at Ellerton University, where Dr. Iverson served as provost. Mr. Barnes, in front of several witnesses, viciously attacked Dr. Iverson on the evening on which the murder was committed. The state will show that sufficient evidence exists so that Mr. Barnes and Ms. Bannister be bound over for trial by their peers, and that, due to the severity of the crime, they be held in the city jail without a posting of bond."

After saying these things, the district attorney sat down.

"Mr. Marsh? The defense?"

Adam rose and spoke in low and comforting tones.

Nina almost wished a jury had been present to hear them.

"Your honor, the defense will do, and needs do, little more than paint a picture of the two people who, completely innocent of any crime at all, sit here accused before you. It will point out that Ms. Bannister is one of the leading citizens of the city of Bay St. Lucy, a teacher and principal there for decades. She is in town because she won Ellerton's first Golden Age Teaching award, which has brought her here to share her teaching expertise with the faculty and student body of Ellerton University. She is a political leader, having formed the well known Lissie movement, and she was instrumental in preventing a possible ecological disaster that might have destroyed the off-shore drilling rig known as Aquatica. She has never, ever, committed a crime of any kind. As for Mr. Barnes, there are few people in town who are more respected. He has been a first-rate journalist here for years. He was nowhere near his house when the murder took place. In point of fact, he was having a quiet glass of wine at a well known wine bar, with Ms. Bannister at the time. We, the defense, do not know how Dr. Iverson came to be in Mr. Barnes' house, but the prosecution doesn't either, and the bottom line is that nothing exists here except circumstantial evidence. There are no fingerprints on the murder weapon. There are no witnesses. No, your honor, the fact is that these two people should be released on bond, and the police department should set about finding out who really shot this unfortunate man."

And, so saying, Adam Marsh sat down.

The judge:

"Prosecution's first witness?"

"Your honor, we'd like to hear from Ms. Barbara Richardson."

"All right, will the bailiff bring in Ms. Richardson?"

Marsh frowned.

"What could she have to say?" whispered Nina.

But he merely shook his head.

Barbara Richardson entered and sat down at the witness table.

"You are Ms. Barbara Richardson?"

"I am."

"What is your occupation, Ms. Richardson?"

"I am CEO of Adornher, a cosmetics firm based in Vicksburg, Mississippi. I also have the honor to serve as chairman of the board of directors of Ellerton University."

"And it is in connection with these duties that you were in our city yesterday."

"Yes. The board convened for its monthly meeting an ten a.m."

"And what happened approximately one hour before that meeting?"

"The president summarily dismissed the full-time faculty as well as the entire administration."

"And how did the board react to this?"

"We were shocked, as everyone was. But rather than dismiss President Herndon immediately—which we thought might have added to an already chaotic situation—we simply implored her to wait, to reconsider her actions."

"And she did not do so."

"No. She called a meeting of all adjunct faculty, to whom she offered what were, in essence, full-time contracts."

"And she had no power to do this?"

"Of course not. And, I might add, it was all done without the board's knowledge."

"And how did Dr. Charles Iverson react to this?"

"He was at a meeting in Hattiesburg. We called him immediately, of course, and he was shocked. He insisted that we hold a massive gathering last night at the stadium, in order to explain to the general public that the stories they were reading in *The Gazette* and on the AP wire were completely without foundation."

"These were stories Mr. Barnes had written."

"Yes, they were."

"What happened at the meeting?"

"Dr. Herndon somehow managed to appear via the Jumbotron screen and announce a tuition cut of fifty percent. This was met with wild applause by the parents and students, and the entire event degenerated into chaos. The board was unable to make clear to the public that such a cut would be completely impossible, and that President Herndon was acting irrationally and needed to be, in fact had officially been, replaced by Provost Iverson."

"Can you talk about the events that transpired just before the announcement you have described?"

"Yes. Provost Iverson and I held an impromptu meeting with several reporters, telling them essentially just what I've told you, and about how the university was planning to proceed."

"Was Mr. Barnes present?"

"Yes. Unfortunately."

"How so?"

"When I attempted to describe what happened at the board meeting, he became enraged and called me a liar. He was, I assume, attempting to defend the veracity of the bizarre stories he had been writing. Dr. Iverson attempted to point out to him the damage his tales had done to the academic community."

"Did Dr. Iverson threaten to have him fired?"

"Yes. He also told him of the university's plans...plans that are already being carried out—to sue *The Gazette*."

"Was Ms. Bannister present?"

"Yes. She was embracing Mr. Barnes."

"Did you have the impression that the two of them were lovers?"

Marsh:

"Objection!"

The judge:

"Sustained."

And, to the prosecutor:

"Let's leave that for now."

"Very well, your honor. But Ms. Richardson, can you tell us what happened next?"

"Mr. Barnes attacked the provost. The two men scuffled for several seconds before security police could get them apart."

"All right. And after the fight was over, you went into the stadium."

"Yes."

"Did either you or the provost see Mr. Barnes and Ms. Bannister again?"

"No. I don't know where they went or what they did."

"But you did hear from them? Or at least you heard from Mr. Barnes?"

Marsh leaned over and whispered to Nina:

"What's he talking about?"

She shook her head:

"I have no idea."

Barbara Richardson:

"It was about twenty minutes after the Jumbotron speech. The provost and I were still outside the stadium, calling as many people as we could, to try to undo the damage the president had done. Suddenly, a young man—probably a student—ran up to us and gave a folded sheet of paper to the provost, saying that he had been asked by Mr. Barnes to deliver this message. I could see the provost's face begin to turn red. I heard him hiss the words, 'If you write that, Barnes, you—' He said an obscenity then."

"I understand."

"But he went on to say, 'If you write that, I'll kill you!'"

There was silence in the courtroom.

Rick, dumbfounded, was simply shaking his head.

"And then, Ms. Richardson?"

"The provost walked away, fast. I never saw him alive again."

A pause. Then the judge:

"Mr. Marsh, do you have any questions for this witness?"

Adam shook his head:

"Not at this time, your honor. Reserve the right to recall."

"Very well. Mr. Prosecutor, your next witness."

"We call Officer Robert Swinton of the city police force."

A young, uniformed, blonde man entered the room, and took his place at the witness chair.

"You are Officer Robert B. Swinton?"

"Yes, I am."

"Were you called to investigate a shooting last night around ten thirty?"

"Yes, I was."

"Who did you receive the call from?"

"Dispatch. They said they'd just received a call saying that shots had been fired, and they gave us the address. My partner and I answered the call, and another unit joined us, pulling up to the door of the house just as we were. The door of the house was closed, but we could see two people standing inside. We called out to them to open the door, but for a time they did nothing. Finally, one of them, the woman, did what we asked, and we entered the premises."

"Are the two people you spoke of here today?"

"Yes, sir, they are seated here at the two tables beside you."

"Let the record show that the witness has referred to Mr. Richard Barnes and Ms. Nina Bannister. Now, Officer, will you go on and tell us what you discovered in the room?"

"We found the body of the man we later learned was Provost at Ellerton University."

"He was dead?"

"Yes. His chest had been blown apart."

"And the murder weapon?"

"It was lying beside the couch; a twenty gauge shotgun."

"What else did you find in the room, after a more thorough search?"

"Sir, on a desk not too far from the sofa, a computer had been set up. It was open and turned on, and the screen was easily visible. I ignored it for some minutes, because so much else was happening in the house."

"I understand. Go on."

"But finally, I decided that whatever was on the screen might have some relevance to the case, because it seemed to have been written by the occupant of the house. So I went over and read it. After reading it, I decided that it certainly was relevant. A printer was hooked up beside the computer, so I printed off the document, which was a letter. Then I made sure that the computer got taken downtown as evidence."

Adam Marsh:

"You had no warrant to search the house, Officer, is that correct?"

Prosecutor:

"Officer, did you not say that the computer was in plain sight?"

"Yes, sir. You couldn't miss it."

"And the letter that apparently had just been written on it, did you make copies of that letter?"

"Later on in the evening, yes, sir."

"Are these the copies that I'm holding in my hand?"

"I believe they are."

"All right. I'm going to pass these around. Your honor, here's one for the court. Mr. Marsh, here's one for the defense. I'll keep one myself. Your honor, permission to read this letter aloud to the court."

Marsh:

"Objection, we do not know how this document was obtained nor have we had a chance to examine it beforehand."

The judge:

"You've just heard how it was obtained. Perfectly legally, since the computer was there in plain sight.

And you're getting a chance to examine it right now, as we all are. Read the document."

The prosecuting attorney adjusted his glasses, cleared his throat, and read:

"*The Gazette* has recently learned that Dr. Charles Iverson, provost of Ellerton University, has been engaged for almost a year in a complex scheme of embezzlement and money laundering, siphoning huge sums of money from the university's retirement fund, and secreting it in an offshore account in the Cayman Islands. The sum involved appears to be more than twenty-five million dollars, and the provost was able to obtain the funds for his own use by means of a complex scheme in which university financial officers as well as board members thought the money was being invested in conservative stocks and bonds. Mr. Iverson's fraud was so cleverly carried out that even the most careful examinations were not able to—"

The prosecutor stopped, then put down the letter.

Nina looked at Rick's face, which had not changed, and still remained frozen in an expression of shock.

Finally, he shook his head and whispered:

"This is insane. I never wrote such a thing."

The judge:

"Defendant will refrain from speaking."

Silence for a time.

Finally, the prosecutor:

"Your honor. Our theory of the crime should now be quite obvious. The message that the young man delivered to the provost was clearly the story appearing on the computer, or at least the partial story. Mr. Barnes was enraged at the provost for threatening a major lawsuit, and also threatening to have him fired from his job at *The Gazette*. He thought if he could create this scandal, the furor would in some strange manner put the provost in the spotlight and make it look as though the provost were on a witch hunt. But more: he hated the man so much, that he wanted to cause as much pain as possible by showing him the story in advance. He probably knew that the provost would be enraged, and even come looking for Mr. Barnes. When the provost arrived, things got out of hand. The provost is a big man, he may have intimidated Mr. Barnes. What actually happened, we may not know for some time. But as for sufficient evidence—your honor, we have the murder weapon, and, even though it has been wiped clean of prints, it unquestionably belongs to Mr. Barnes. We have the fight earlier in the evening; we have the testimony of Mrs. Richardson, who saw the document delivered; we have Ms. Richardson's memory of the provost—outraged—in as much as saying he was going after Mr. Barnes; and we have the document itself, just as it had been written, obviously by Mr. Barnes, and on his own word processor."

He paused, then said:

"Of course, your honor, this is not a trial. We have no way of knowing whether Mr. Barnes' allegations concerning financial misconduct are accurate. We do know that the two men hated each other, and that somehow they clashed in Mr. Barnes' house, at a time when Mr. Barnes was there with a woman who seems to have been his mistress. Could this be a case of self defense? Possibly. Was it a crime of passion in some way? Also a possibility, and we will not know the truth of it until we get the truth out of the surviving witnesses. But sufficient evidence? Of course, there is. And so we move that these two defendants be bound over and held, without bail, awaiting trial."

The judge:

"Mr. Marsh, both of these defendants are, I believe, your clients?"

"Yes, your honor."

"Statements?"

"Rick, you go first."

"All right."

Rick walked to the witness table. He spoke quietly, his voice shaking somewhat.

"I have no idea what could have happened in my house last night. None of this makes any sense to me, any sense at all. Yes, I covered the assembly at the stadium and yes, the provost and I had a fight. He said my reports concerning what went on at the board meeting were inaccurate, and, worse still, that they were lies. They weren't lies. They were entirely accurate. The board *was* shocked to find out what President Herndon had done, and they were about to vote for her dismissal. But Peter Stockton bribed them with the offer of millions of dollars in donations and fifty acres of prime land. They decided to do nothing at all, and simply wait to see if Lucinda Herndon's revolution—and that's what it is, a revolution—would be successful. I reported those things, just as they happened. When the provost attacked me, all right, I attacked him back. Then the meeting at the stadium happened. I covered it, wrote a story about it, and sent it to *The Gazette*. Then Ms. Bannister—we had been together all this time—parted, because she received an invitation to dine at the residence with President Herndon. That is where she went, and that is where she was from approximately eight until ten p.m., when we met at a wine bar."

"What did you do between eight and ten?"

"I just walked. I'm sorry, I don't remember exactly where I walked."

"Did you see anyone?"

"Of course, there are always students around, walking on campus."

"You didn't speak to anyone?"

"No, I was—just kind of lost in my own thoughts."

A pause.

Then:

"Mr. Barnes, this is going to come out eventually. It might as well come out now. What were you thinking about? What was occupying your mind to the extent that it pretty much blocked out everything else?"

Rich was silent for a time, and finally looked at Nina.

She nodded.

And he said:

"I had met Ms. Bannister only a day or so before. We found ourselves together during the remarkable events of yesterday. I guess we found that we were developing feelings for each other. I was debating whether, at the wine bar on Hacker Street, I would ask her to come home with me, and spend the night with me."

"And what did you decide?"

"I decided to ask her, and she said yes."

"And so the two of you walked together back to your house."

"Yes."

"Which you entered, and in which you saw the provost's body?"

"That's right."

"You did not write the document that has been shown to the court?"

"I've never seen such a document."

"You know nothing about a financial scam being perpetrated by the provost?"

"Nothing at all. Even hearing about such a thing comes as a complete shock to me."

"You sent him no message, warning him that you were about to expose him?"

"No. I was thinking about other things."

"About Ms. Bannister."

"Yes."

"All right, Rick, that's all."

He returned to his seat.

And it was her turn.

It was as though she stepped out of her body and watched another human being walk the six steps to the witness table.

But there she was.

She had, she knew, a much better situation than Rick.

She had an alibi.

So she found it somewhat easier to say:

"Mr. Barnes has pretty much told you all there is to say. I was with him at the stadium. I saw the fight and saw him write the story about what happened in the stadium. And yes, we parted. And yes, we had developed feelings for each other. He told me he needed to walk for a time. I knew what he was wondering about. I was wondering about it, too. But it was easier for me, because I was eating a late supper with President Herndon. She told me about her ideas in a bit more depth, and she asked me if I would accept a job she had mentioned earlier in the day. I told her I would take the job."

"And that job was?"

"Locating more retired teachers—truly excellent teachers—who would come and spend a semester at Ellerton."

"And what time did you leave the residence?"

"About ten minutes before ten."

"And then?"

"I walked to the wine bar. I had a glass of wine with Rick—with Mr. Barnes. He asked me if I would go to bed with him, and I said yes. Then we left together, walked back to Mr. Barnes' house, and discovered the body."

"Do you have anything more to say, Ms. Bannister?"

"No, that's all."

"All right, then, you may stand down."

She did so.

The judge:

"More witnesses, Mr. Marsh?"

"Yes, your honor. Defense calls Lucinda Herndon."

Lucinda entered the room, impeccably dressed in a dark red suit. She walked briskly to the witness table and sat down.

"Dr. Herndon, you are president of Ellerton University?"

"I am."

"Do you know both Richard Barnes and Nina Bannister?"

"I know them both and have great respect for each of them."

"How long have you known Ms. Bannister?"

"For more than forty years. We were students together."

"Did you invite her to come and teach for a semester at Ellerton?"

"Yes. She was the first winner of the Golden Age Teaching Award. I chose her myself."

"And you did this, I assume, both because of her teaching ability and because of her character, her integrity."

"That is correct."

"Now, let's get to last night. You gave, I believe, a closed-circuit address to a large group of people assembled at the stadium."

"Yes. I told the group about our plan to cut tuition. They were quite excited."

"Fine. After the address was done, you dispatched a student to deliver a message to Ms. Bannister, inviting her to the residence for a late dinner."

Lucinda Herndon said nothing.

Tell them, Nina found herself thinking.

Tell them.

Marsh continued:

"She arrived shortly before nine o'clock. The two of you had sherry together, then went into the dining room for a late supper of oysters. Ms. Bannister left shortly before ten to join Mr. Barnes at the wine bar on Hatcher Street. So we need you simply to confirm that, at the time the provost was killed, Ms. Bannister was eating dinner with you."

Nothing from Lucinda.

Tell them, Lucinda.

Tell them!

Finally, Lucinda Herndon shook her head and, looking first at Rick and then at Nina, said:

"I'm sorry. Both of you. I know what you want me to say. Mister Marsh told me, Nina, of your need for my assistance here today. And I have struggled with my feelings concerning this matter."

Nina, despite herself, rose in her chair and half shouted:

"For God's sakes, Lucinda, tell them where I was last night!"

But there was only another shake of the head.

And Lucinda Herndon, looking solemnly at the judge, said:

"I cannot lie about this matter. I must tell you all the truth. Which is that I never saw Ms. Bannister at any time last night."

Nina, stunned, slumped into her chair.

There was complete silence in the courtroom.

CHAPTER EIGHTEEN: OLD WHITTINGTON

This could not be happening. There was a dreamlike quality about the entire scene. For a certain number of seconds Lucinda Herndon remained motionless, her expression stone-like, her eyes staring straight in front of her. She nodded when told she was excused, and she walked purposely from the courtroom, not looking right nor left, and acting as though neither Nina nor Rick even existed.

More silence.

Finally, Adam Marsh said, quietly to the judge:

"Your honor, I'd like a moment to confer with my clients before the court takes any action."

A nod.

"I can understand your position, Mr. Marsh. Why don't you take them into examination room B?"

"Thank you."

A moment later, they were seated around a small table in a windowless room.

Nina wondered for an instant if the rest of her life was to be lived at small tables in windowless rooms.

This could not be happening. What was going on in Lucinda's mind?

When the three of them were seated as comfortably as could be expected under the circumstances, Adam Marsh looked sternly at both of them and said:

"What is going on here?"

Neither answered for a time. Finally, Nina said:

"She's lying."

Marsh:

"Why?"

"I don't know, Mr. Marsh. I can only tell you that I am not lying. I was there. I drank the sherry, I ate the oysters. I listened to her talk about the stupidity of the research that was going on. Toward the end of our time together, she quoted Margaret Mead. We held hands. We even talked about Rick."

"She knew about your relationship?"

"She had guessed it. I told her he was probably going to ask me to go to bed with him and I was probably going to say yes. I told her I was going to accept the job she was offering me. Mr. Marsh, I did not dream these things."

"If Nina says this dinner happened, Adam, then it happened."

Marsh simply shook his head.

"Now both of you have to listen to me. I'm as good a lawyer as you're likely to get. But I can't do miracles. Whatever actually happened, we can make a defense. If the provost was actually embezzling money, Rick, and you found out about it—"

"But he wasn't embezzling money, at least as far as I know!"

"Did you tell anybody at *The Gazette* about this story you were working on?"

"No, dammit, because there was no story!"

"Then what about Richardson's testimony?"

"It makes no sense."

"I'm only saying, Rick, that the testimony we've heard is truly damning. And Ms. Bannister—"

He turned to Nina:

"Either the president is lying—which seems highly improbable—or she's—"

He shook his head:

"I don't know. I don't know any other possibility. I can only say that, if the provost came to your house last night, Rick, and the two of you fought, with Nina present."

"That did not happen!"

"No. What did happen was that you walked for two hours and can't even remember where, and Nina ate ghost oysters with one of the most intelligent and respected women in the state—and she swears you weren't anywhere near her. Great."

Silence for a time.

Marsh:

"You're both sticking with these stories?"

Nina and Rick nodded.

Finally, Rick said, quietly:

"Adam, if you'd like us to get somebody else—"

"No, there isn't anybody else. No lawyer in town would be crazy enough to take this case, and the public defender is not much more than a kid. You've got me and that's all. But if I find out you're lying, I'm gone. I won't be lied to."

"Mr. Marsh," said Nina, "I had the dinner. I swear to God."

"Well, that's exactly who you'll be swearing to. Okay. You both have to realize that they're probably going to bind you over. Peter Stockton is a powerful man and he's got a lot of both money and influence to spread around. But not enough. Not in the face of Herndon's testimony."

"We understand," said Rick.

"All right then. Let's go back in there and take our medicine."

They rose.

Rick walked up to her and said:

"I'm sorry about this, Nina. I'm sorry I got you into it."

She shook her head:

"I'm not. I'm in my late sixties and thought I wasn't going to have, ever again, the feelings I've had for you. But I have them and I'm not ashamed of them. As for the other things, they're impossible. There's no way to explain them. They're like a bad novel written by a lunatic or a drunk. But they aren't your fault, Rick. We may be the only two people in this insane world who know the truth; but I'm not sorry I got to know Rick Barnes, and I never will be."

He smiled at her, seemingly unable to speak, and he nodded:

"Let's go," said Adam Marsh.

And they did.

They'd seated themselves in their original positions when the judge, looking first at one and then the other, began to speak:

"Ms. Bannister; Mr. Barnes; Mr. Marsh. I've heard the testimony, and have listened with as much sympathy as possible. But in light of what we've heard here this morning, the court has no choice other than—"

The door opened and a police officer, a tall blonde woman, entered:

"Your honor, I'm sorry for the interruption! But something has come up."

The judge looked up:

"What has come up?"

"Another witness."

"What are you talking about?"

"A man—a professor at the university, I think—is saying that he has something extremely important to say to the court."

The prosecutor, shaking his head:

"I don't see why he's waited so long. We interviewed everybody who seems to know anything about this. Your honor, I think you ought to tell him to—
—"

But the judge cut him off:

"No. This has all just happened. Nobody has had time to interview all witnesses who might be vital, to either side. No, I'm going to allow him to come in and talk to us, especially if defense has no objections."

Marsh:

"None your honor."

"All right, bring in this professor, and let's see what he's got to say."

The officer disappeared for a second.

Then a small and dapper man entered. Nina recognized him immediately as the classics professor who'd taken her, two nights previously, to the university library.

"You are, sir?"

"Whittington."

"Have a seat."

"Thank you. And thank you for hearing what I have to say."

"It's our duty to hear it, just as it's your duty to bring it to us. That is, if it's truly important."

"It is. It's not pretty. But it's important."

"All right. Your occupation?"

"I'm a full professor of classics here at Ellerton. Have been my entire career, more than forty years."

"And why have you come forward here?"

"I was outside, in the crowd. I talked to Lucinda when she was leaving."

"President Herndon?"

"Yes. Lucinda and I have been close for decades. I knew her husband, Thomas, quite well. At any rate, she told me just then, just outside there, that she was not going to lie for anyone, not even for her old friend, Ms. Bannister."

"The president was not authorized to discuss her testimony with anyone."

"Well, nevertheless she did. And as soon as she did, why, I realized what I had to do."

"Which was?"

"Say some very unpleasant, even tragic, things."

"They will not be the first unpleasant or tragic things we've heard here this morning. So go ahead."

"All right. Last week I had dinner with the president. She invites me over to the residence, usually once a month. We rehash old times."

"Go on."

"She began telling me at length about her plans to fire the faculty and administration. She swore me to secrecy. I was stunned, of course, but, as she went on, I could see that she was making sense. And I even found myself agreeing with her. Why, when I began here as a young professor, we were proud of our profession. The profession of college teaching. Never, never, would we have allowed into these classrooms college-level teachers who were paid the miserable wages these adjuncts are given. We would have gone on strike before letting that happen. And as for administrators, there were only eight of them. And that's all. Now…it's insane, and she was right to see that."

"All right, Mr. Whittington, but the court doesn't quite see…"

"And so I agreed with her, and told her I agreed with her. She merely smiled. Then she walked around the table, took my hand, squeezed it firmly, and said: 'Of course, you agree with it. Because after all, it's your vision, Thomas. Your vision entirely. Now I feel a bit tired. Let's go to bed.' And, after saying these things, she turned and left the room."

Silence for a time.

The judge:

"She called you…"

"Thomas."

"She thought you were her husband?"

"Yes. I'm sure of it."

"What did you do after she'd left the room?"

"I went home. I was very shaken."

"I can understand."

"But the next evening, on some excuse, I went by the residence. To check on her. She met me at the main door, embraced me, told me it had been too long, and that I must come over for dinner sometime."

Silence in the room. Several deep breaths.

The prosecutor:

"You're saying she'd forgotten that you were there at all?"

"Yes."

"Oh, my God."

"I know. I said that phrase several times in the next few days. But I tried to dismiss it as a one time occurrence. I knew I should say something to someone, but wasn't able to bring myself to do so. I did manage to find excuses to drop by during the next couple of days. She always seemed fine, alert. But the important thing is this: one of the times I dropped by was last night. I wanted to congratulate her on her splendid victory."

"What time did you go by, Professor Whittington?"

"It must have been around nine thirty. I walked across the yard to the side entrance of the residence. But I did not go up to the door and knock."

"Because?"

"I could see through the window, and into the dining room. She was having a guest for dinner."

"And that guest was?"

"Ms. Bannister."

So saying, he looked down at the floor.

Nina should, she realized, have been ecstatic.

Instead, she felt like crying.

CHAPTER NINETEEN: VISITS FROM FRIENDS

The alibi offered by Whittington of Classics—aided no doubt by the man's general bearing and demeanor—proved effective. It set in motion events that were to encircle Lucinda Herndon, who, if it were to be proven true, might very well be suffering from early stages of Alzheimer's, and Nina Bannister, who, if it were to be proven true, was nowhere near Rick Bannister's house at the time a murder was being committed.

In short, it allowed for Nina to be released from police custody after some hours time, her bond provided by the benevolent Peter Stockton.

He was, in fact, the first person she saw as she approached the exit to the police station, on her way to she knew not where.

Actually, she found herself thinking, it did not matter very much where; she simply needed to get out of there.

"Peter, how can I ever thank you?"

He shook his head:

"I didn't think it was going to work there for a while. I have a lot of dirt on a lot of people, but when I heard that Lucinda had denied your being there..."

"I know. It was a nightmare. I thought I was losing my mind."

"You're not. But from what the word now seems to be..."

"I know. When Professor Whittington told his story I should have been excited. But I was crushed. She had seemed so lucid during the last days, brilliant even. Now I don't know. Is the word out?"

"Yes."

"What are they going to do?"

"What they have to do. Have her examined. Probably removed as president."

"I'm sure that's what the faculty and administrators want. But Peter, what about Rick? Can you get him out now?"

A shake of the head.

"Unfortunately, Lucinda's mental condition doesn't have much bearing on his part of the case. There's still so much that's going against him. He can't say where he was. Too many people saw that attack at the stadium. And there's Barbara Richardson's testimony about the message he got. There's also the damned message itself, if you really think about it, sitting there on Rick's word processor."

"But Rick insists he didn't write that message!"

"I know, Ms. Bannister, and I believe the man. But the bottom line is, I can't get him out. I did get you out, though. Question is, where do you want to go?"

"I want to go back to my Hobbit House, and sit in the little yard, and drink some tea, and just think of what I can do to help Rick. Do you think that's possible?"

He nodded.

"Might otherwise be tough, but contacts help. We can sneak you out the back. I've hired some private security people who can kind of keep a lookout on the place to be sure no crowd of reporters comes looking for a story."

"Let's go then."

They did, and Peter Stockton was as good as his word.

They wove through a tangle of back alleys and small streets, the limousine almost too large to get through in some instances.

Finally, she saw the little red roof of the house shining crimson through thick magnolia leaves.

As she got out of the car, reveling in warm, fresh air, she felt a sense of wonder.

How many centuries had passed since she'd left here, walking to Lucinda's Residence, in preparation for her first faculty meeting?

Several lifetimes, certainly.

But really, when one thought about it, not much had actually happened.

Lucinda had fired the faculty and all the administration. Then she and Rick had attended the board meeting, where Peter Stockton had bribed the leadership of the entire university with a billion or so dollars of money and land. Then there had been the adjunct meeting, where five hundred or so characters who could have come straight out of Dickens' London—the poor parts—had learned that they now had careers and, instead of teaching remedial English, were to start running the university and be paid for it. Then she'd been taken to Rick's lake house, realizing that, somewhere amid all the events that had happened that morning, she was completing the process of falling in love with him.

But that was about it.

Nothing more happened except the incredible scene at the stadium and the ghost oyster dinner with Lucinda and the wine bar "let's go to bed" Chardonnay, and the near going to bed except that one could not because of the corpse on the sofa. And the being arrested and the getting sprung and the sleeping pill from Lucinda and the preliminary trial and hopelessness and then finally hope…

…except that such hope depended on the realization that her old and dear friend was losing her mind.

Yep. That was about all that had happened.

Strange that she felt tired, drained.

Peter Stockton opened the gate and let her walk through it.

The door to the cottage opened and Adam Marsh walked out, smiling.

"Welcome home!"

She walked quickly up to him and embraced him.

"Adam. I might have known you'd be waiting for me."

"Seemed the least I could do. Door wasn't locked."

She shook her head:

"Didn't seem like there was a need. I don't have anything important in there. Adam, how is Rick?"

"He's all right. He's ecstatic about your being cleared. And at the same time, he's crushed about Lucinda. As we all are. I think those things are more important to him than his own case. But we can talk about that later. Nina, I have to tell you, I'm not alone here."

His smile vanished.

What was he talking about?

Who was waiting for her?

Who could not be put off?

What was she going to have to deal with now?

"There's a pair waiting for you in there that wouldn't be denied."

"Who?"

"You're going to have to find that out for yourself. Just realize there was not very much I could do about it."

Everyone was silent for a while.

Finally, she squared her shoulders and took a deep breath.

"All right, Adam. Whoever they are, let's deal with them."

So saying, she walked past Marsh and through the door.

A huge figure stood before her, beaming.

"Jackson! Jackson Bennett!"

"Hello, Nina. Bay St. Lucy asked me to give you their best. We all miss you, Nina! But nobody as much as this guy!"

He pointed to a small chair, from the cushion of which was descending a small, tan and white animal.

"Furl! Oh, Furl, you've come to visit me!"

But Furl merely sauntered across the room, rubbed against her ankle in one direction, turned and rubbed back against it in another, and said:

"Aaarrrgggh."

Which in cat means:

"So what have you gotten yourself into this time?"

CHAPTER TWENTY: THE DARK SUN

When Jackson Bennett entered a room, he became the dark sun around which everything else in the space orbited. Here in the middle of Nina's Hobbit House, his darkness was belied by the brilliant celestial light that was his smile, while his mass held in regular and fixed orbits Adam, Mars, Nina, Venus, Peter Stockton, Jupiter, and Furl—a declawed asteroid that had landed on the surface of Nina.

Their little universe chugged along, ultimately smelling of fresh hot coffee and problem-solving minds.

"I wasn't sure you were coming," Nina said.

Jackson merely shrugged (as though any movement of his mammoth shoulders might be signified by a term such as *merely*.)

"I was in such a hurry to get up here," he rumbled. "I guess I just disconnected, grabbed Furl and hit the road. Sorry if I worried you."

"I'm just glad you're here."

Jackson bent forward:

"Nina, we're worried about you, you know that."

"I'm worried about me, too."

Peter Stockton:

"All right then. Can anybody tell me what's being done to get Mr. Barnes out of jail? Because I've done all I can do, and he's still sitting there."

To which, Adam Marsh replied:

"First things first. I think I ought to tell the two of you that Mr. Bennett here and myself are now *both* actively involved in the case. Richard agreed to have us as co-counsel about an hour ago; we hope you'll go along with the same agreement."

"I can't pay either of you."

"Neither can he, so it's okay."

"Well," she said, stroking a dubious Furl, "as long as that's taken care of. I didn't want there to be any bothersome financial details."

"That only happens," said Jackson, "when there's money involved."

"If you gentlemen wish to be paid—and paid well," Peter Stockton said, "then I and my associates can…"

Marsh shook his head:

"You're just as impossible for us to deal with as Nina. She has too little money and you have too much. We don't have software that can deal with that many zeros. One transaction with you would break down our whole accounting system."

"All right then. I'm just saying…"

"Don't worry about it, Pete. But as for the other thing you were saying, about Barnes and his getting out—well, the whole investigation right now is centered furiously on the university's financial situation."

Stockton nodded:

"Those accusations, you mean, about the provost embezzling money."

"Those are the ones. Jackson and I have been pulling every string we can. He's got more of them because he has contacts in the governor's office, and the governor's office has contacts deep in the university's financial world. All of the people who handle the money, and who make any investments that are to be made. As far as we can find out—and remember, all this broke little more than a few hours ago, so nothing too exhaustive has been done yet—is that it's impossible."

"What is?" growled Stockton.

"The kind of embezzlement scheme Rick's article—or let's just say *the* article, because somebody sure as hell wrote it—accused the provost of working out. He couldn't have done it. He never had that kind of financial access."

"That," said Nina, "would square with Rick's story. If Rick wrote that the provost was stealing money, then that would be true. But he never wrote it."

"And still," grumbled Stockton, "he's behind bars. And he doesn't deserve it. Hell, he's not the one that's liberal. He just writes what they tell him to write. Okay, so tell me about something else."

"Name it," said Marsh.

"What's happening with the university?"

Marsh shook his head:

"Nobody really knows, but it's a mess. While Lucinda was, well—in control—it really did seem that she had a chance of winning. A great many people, not only here in Ellerton but around the country, were supporting her. And only a shockingly small number were supporting a hundred and fifty thousand dollar a year Assistant Directors of Planning Design and Research Marketing."

"What is that?" asked Jackson Bennett.

Marsh answered:

"Something that you put a suit around and give money to."

Stockton:

"But now?"

"Now, Peter, the other side has learned about Lucinda's—situation."

"Her possible situation," Nina said. "We don't know that she's ill."

"True, Nina, but if she isn't ill, then you weren't eating oysters with her. And if that's the case, then it follows that..."

"I hate," Nina said, quietly, "logic."

Jackson Bennett:

"That's all right, Nina. As far as I can tell, it doesn't seem to apply to what's been happening here at dear old Ellerton."

Marsh:

"At any rate, it comes down to this: if the contracts Lucinda gave out are considered legally binding—then a great many people have been let go into early retirement, not all of them being unhappy about the situation. But if they're not—and they're *not* if she's mentally incapacitated—then this whole thing has been a farce. Adjuncts are still adjuncts, and Vice Directors of Global Awareness and Cultural Enrichment are still what they are, whatever they are."

"My God," said Stockton.

Marsh nodded:

"There are hundreds of lawyers working on this thing as we speak. It's like I said—a mess."

Silence for a time. Then Nina:

"Adam, Jackson—and you too, Peter: there are two things most important to me right now. First, I know I didn't shoot the man. And I know just as strongly that Richard Barnes didn't either."

"All right," said Jackson Bennett. "So where does that leave us?"

"It leaves us," said Nina, "asking who did. If Barbara Richardson is right, and I can't believe she would be wrong about a thing like this, *someone* delivered a message to the provost. He read it and became infuriated. He went to Rick's house and was shot. Now the question is, by *whom*? Someone got into Rick's house and typed that letter on the word processor, somehow got a copy of the same letter over to the stadium, then, knowing that Rick had a shotgun there, just sat there and waited for the provost."

"Could all that have actually happened?" asked Marsh.

"If you eliminate everything impossible," said Nina quietly, "whatever remains, no matter how bizarre, must be the truth. Conan Doyle."

More silence.

Finally, Jackson Bennett:

"You said there were two things, Nina, that were important to you now."

"Yes."

"What's the other?"

She looked around the room, then said:

"I want to see Rick."

The visiting area of the city jail looked like any number of bureaucratic spaces. There were gray tables, gray metal chairs, gray walls, gray pictures on the walls, and gray people coming and going on gray errands.

The officers all resembled mail carriers except they had guns.

Nina was signed in, said a quick farewell to the three men who'd brought her, and followed the armed mailwoman assigned to her along a winding series of corridors.

Finally, she entered the large room that was the visitation area.

She was told to sit at a non-descript table in the middle of the room. She looked around her. Most of the other tables were vacant, but there were two or three other visitations taking place. The room had been divided into two parts by a ceiling to floor glass partition. Free people sat on one side of it, prisoners the other. To her left, she saw a middle-aged and harried-looking blond woman reach up to touch the glass, several inches behind which was the face of her husband.

An officer observing the event grunted something, and shook his head.

Other than this small drama, not much was happening in the visiting area.

Until Rick entered the room from a door tucked into a corner far behind the glass wall.

She caught her breath.

Not because he smiled at her upon entering, nor because he was wearing a bright orange jump suit like she'd seen work-gang prisoners wear. But because he looked so completely at ease, moving with a gentle, slightly stooped grace across the room toward her.

She stood up, noticing that two officers had stationed themselves on either side of her.

Rick was brought to the wall. He sat down.

So did she.

For a time, he simply sat there, smiling and shaking his head.

What could be said?

Do not discuss the case.

All right.

Then what?

He continued to look at her, probably wondering the same thing.

Finally, she moved an inch or two closer to the glass, took a deep breath, and said, quietly:

"That was the worst first date I ever had in my life."

Both of the officers standing beside her, a man and a woman, broke up laughing.

It took them a while to stop.

There was, after that, only one more thing to say, and she said it:

"I'm going to get you out of here. I'm going to find out who did this thing. And then you'll be out of here."

So saying, she got up, turned, and left the room.

CHAPTER TWENTY ONE: FESTIVAL OF THE FOOLS

A reader of Victor Hugo's *The Hunchback of Notre Dame* will be struck by the experiences of Pierre Gringoire, an unsuccessful writer of Masques, who is kidnapped on New Year's Day, 1491, and carried into the Festival of Fools, a gathering of motley robbers, cutthroats, drunks, and madmen, which takes place annually in the Place de Grève in Paris.

The same reader will see how closely parallel to Gringoire's experiences were those of Nina Bannister, upon her exit from the city jail.

She had attained to within ten feet or so of the Peter Stockton limousine and the three men standing beside it waiting for her—when a Gathering of Fools subsumed her and carried her away in a strange, shouting, tide-like, drunken march that seemed to be moving toward the middle of the campus.

"Nina!"

This from Adam Marsh, who was peering around the bizarrely-clad sea of people surrounding Nina with a sense of panic.

"Nina!"

This from Jackson Bennett.

"Nina!"

This from Peter Stockton.

"Nina! Nina! Nina!"

This from various of the people engulfing her, many of whom seemed to be slightly drunk.

"Come with us! We're all fired!"

She recognized the massive man who'd welcomed her to the table at Nick's following her meeting with the uncountable administrators two interminable days ago.

The huge man put a huge arm around her and shouted in her ear:

"We're all going back to the gym, where Lucinda gave us the contracts two days ago."

"Who?"

"All of us!"

And then she realized. This Feast of the Fools was, in fact, the Feast of the Adjuncts.

They had gathered en masse, just as they had when they were told they would soon be running the university.

And now, apparently, that dream was over.

She wondered as the mob made its way across the campus, a few students laughing as they stared at it, some of them apparently recognizing part-time teachers who'd taught them in past courses—if these multi-aged, multi-ethnicitied, multi-clad, wildly-costumed people had dressed fantastically for this one occasion, this last time for them to come together as true, regularly salaried employees of the university—or if this was simply the way part-timers always dressed, hobo-like and ramshackle.

There were various adjuncts at her side now, some she recognized, others not. They were shouting and singing, here and there a fragment of the school song, the old fight song, and somewhere, from the edge of the crowd, some Latin versus from Gaudeamus Igitor.

The massive man introduced himself:

"When we met at Nick's the other afternoon, I didn't introduce myself. I'm Tom Scott, mathematics."

"Hello, Tom."

"We're glad to have you with us. We heard about all that horror with the provost. Somehow they thought you were involved in it?"

"Yes, they did."

"But you're cleared now. You know about all the other stuff that's been going on?"

She shook her head.

"I know about some things. But in the last few hours so much has happened…"

He nodded:

"We're in the same situation. Rumors, rumors. The bottom line is, they're saying Lucinda is mentally incompetent. She's been replaced by the vice provost. We've all been informed that the contracts offered us are invalid."

"So what are you doing now?"

"What we should have been doing all these years—meeting."

"Do you think you can accomplish anything?"

"Who knows? This is all new. Maybe Lucinda Herndon *is* mentally incompetent, we don't know. But for the first time in most of our *careers*, if you can call them *careers*, an administrator has treated us as though we were better than window washers. Okay, so we can't become full-timers. Okay, so the nine hundred or so bureaucrats will go on and keep their jobs. But we will band together now, and we will show the university what a mess they would be in without us."

Nina looked around her, up at the lacy-clouded Mississippi sky, and, not quite so high but equally impressive, a small sea of hand-painted signs, saying *Adjunct Rights*! and *We Count For Something*! and *On Strike For Better Wages*!

They were approaching the old gym now.

The last time she'd stood in this spot, Rick Barnes had been with her.

She tried to get her mind in order, but failed, miserably.

What was she even doing here in this strange crowd? How did their interests intertwine with hers? She had, or should have, only one job now. It was not to reform a major research university; it was rather to figure out what had actually happened the previous night.

Think, Nina, *think.*

No one else seemed ready and eager to help Rick.

But someone had lured the provost to Rick's house, let him get inside the house, and then shot him.

Surely, the provost had many enemies.

But one of them had managed to get a fake message to him outside the stadium, a message warning of an article that accused him of embezzlement. The message had been left visible on Rick's computer.

But how...

Jane, Jane, Jane Austen:

"A mind lively and at ease can do with seeing nothing, and can see nothing that does not answer."

How could...

How could...

But it would not work. She found herself being captivated by this sea of fools, this mob of adjuncts as they worked their way into the old gymnasium.

They were out of the entry hallway now, working their way into the seats.

Not so far away from her, she saw Tyra, and she remembered the day before, the quote from Milton:

"They anon with hundreds and with thousands trooping came attended: all access was thronged, the gates and porches wide, but chief the spacious hall thick swarmed, as bees in spring time..."

Part-time teachers, now become bees in springtime.

Bees in springtime, teaching the nation's youth.

And making two thousand dollars a course.

The microphone was squawking; she saw Tom Scott, he of massive math, who had disattached himself from her and now stood in the middle of the gym floor, addressing the Feast of Fools:

"All right, people! Some time yesterday, I got word that you had elected me to be the head of this faculty. Ex-faculty."

Voices from the audience:

"Hear! hear!"

And:

"Scott for president!"

And a few catcalls, a few more cheers:

Finally, Scott:

"I guess all of us have heard the same things now. President Herndon is—well, under evaluation."

Silence for a time.

"No one knows the exact status of our contracts, but it doesn't look good. It looks, in fact, as though things are going to revert to the way they were."

"Noooo!"

"Down with the way things were!"

"Up with the adjuncts!"

But Scott merely raised his arms and smiled.

"Take it easy. Whatever is going to happen, as far as I'm concerned, we're *still* the faculty, and we're *still* the administration!"

"Huzzah!"

"Tell it! Tell it!"

Scott:

"So I'm taking time this morning to ask for reports. This may be the last time you get to address your peers. So I need volunteers from the *new* administration. People who will get up here and do an oral status report on your area."

Hands went up. Tom Scott gestured:

"Mary Alexander!"

"I'm here!"

"Come on up to the podium!"

A tall, slender, dark-haired woman strode to the speaker's stand and took the microphone.

"I'm Dr. Mary Alexander. Some of you know me, some don't. I have my Ph.D. from Yale, and I teach two sections of remedial English here. At our last meeting, I assumed the position of Assistant Vice Chancellor for Internal Growth and Development. I wish to inform you all that, as far as I can tell from research I did yesterday afternoon and this morning, we are growing and developing internally at a very nice pace."

"Yes!"

"Yes!"

"Up with Internal Growth and Development!"

It was now Mary Alexander's turn to call for quiet, which she ultimately got.

"I can only say though that there is indeed room for improvement."

"Sure there is!"

"Huzzah for improvement!"

"I can tell you now without fear of being gainsaid, that we have, in my expert administrative opinion, the possibility to attain and maintain not only a healthy state of internal growth and development, but an admirable and consistent level of *external* growth and development!"

Wild cheering at this.

"Yes! Yes! External growth forever!"

To which, Mary Alexander, still appealing for quiet, said over the clamor:

"There is, as far as I can tell, only one major impediment standing in our way. And that is, the size of the Office of Internal Growth and Development is, at present, too limited. We have only a Chancellor for

Internal Growth and Development, a Vice Chancellor for Internal Growth and Development, and my own position, and Assistant Vice Chancellor for Internal Growth and Development. To these few people, as well, of course, as the eight administrative assistants assigned to work with us, fall the entire burden of growing and developing internally. Without additional help, growing externally must remain a—well, a mere pipe dream."

"Nooo!"

"Down with the pipe dream! Bring in more people!"

"I am thus officially submitting, as of this afternoon, if by that time, I am still Assistant Vice Chancellor for Internal Growth and Development, a proposal calling for the creation of a new official: Associate Assistant Vice Chancellor for Internal Growth and Development!"

"Yes!"

"This new associate will associate with me, as I assist the vice chancellor, who assists, of course, the chancellor. As we grow, and as we develop. Not only internally, but externally."

Tom Scott, applauding, as was everyone else in the gym, took the microphone from her and announced:

"An extremely exciting proposal, Mary! The thought that this great university may someday begin to grow externally as well as internally…"

Mary corrected him:

"Grow and develop, Tom."

"Sorry, grow and develop both internally and externally—this boggles the mind. Mary, are there any other universities in the county that are actually doing this currently, growing and developing both internally and externally?"

She took the microphone back and said into it:

"Harvard, Yale, and Stanford."

He took it back.

"What a wonderful group to join!"

"You may know, Tom, that a good many people in Mississippi already refer to Ellerton University as the Harvard of the South."

"I had heard that, Mary. Do you know if many people in Boston refer to Harvard as the Ellerton University of the North?"

"I'm not currently aware of that, Tom. But it's certainly one of the things we shall have to look into, if we are to grow and develop both internally and externally, as our potential newly expanded office seeks to help us do!"

"Wonderful! And now, adjuncts, I suggest that we not make Mary wait. Let's vote right now! All in favor of creating the new administrative position of Associate Assistant Vice Chancellor of Growth and Development say *aye!*"

Raucous response:

Aye!

Aye!

Damned right! Aye it is!

And finally, Tom Scott:

"The *ayes* have it; the office is created. The job pays ten dollars a year. Who wants it?"

"*I do!*"

"*No, I do!*"

"*Pick me! Pick me!*"

Scott:

"Eenie meenie, mynie moe—*You!*"

"*Yes!*"

"What's your name?"

"William Alexander!"

"What's your background, Bill?"

"Chemical engineering, Ph.D. from MIT."

"And what do you teach here?"

"Remedial math, one section, hope to get a second one in the spring."

"Of course you do! What do you know about internal and external growth and development, Bill?"

"My wife is pregnant. There's a lot of internal development now, but we hope it will become mostly external development."

"You've got the job!"

"Thank you! Thank you all!"

"Great. And now: we're going to hear from a few more administrators. I know I can count on reports from the Assistant Vice President for Financial Services, the Assistant Vice President for Administrative Services, the Director of Operational Review, the Associate Vice-Director for Operational and Contractual Services, the Assistant Vice President for Financial Services—and many others. We'd like to hear from all nine hundred or so of you, of course, but time constrains us. What we do want to do now is invite a special person to the podium. Before this person comes down, I'd like to say that all of us hope President Herndon's appointments remain valid. But if they don't, there is a chance that, by the end of the day, we will move from being aristocrats— real, full-time professors at the university—to fools, adjuncts who scurry around like rats, trying to cobble together livings in academia's alleyways and sewers."

"*All right then!*"

"*Up the rats*!'

"If that happens, there's one person we've only recently met, that we want to invite to join our ranks. We want to make her an official adjunct. Because we'd be happy to have her as one of us. And so I invite to the podium—*Ms. Nina Bannister!*"

Shocked, she sat for a time.

Then she found herself at the podium.

Along with Tyra, who was holding out her arms and offering her something.

What was it?

Then she realized.

"We all wanted you to have this," said Tyra, "in honor of Nick's and so you'll always be an adjunct and remember us part-timers."

She reached out for it.

"Thank you so much! Thank you so much!"

"You have to read the note, too."

She clutched it to her.

It was furry and about a foot in circumference.

It was a green frog.

She read the note:

"If I have to show you this one more time…"

And she was an adjunct.

CHAPTER TWENTY TWO: THE PERSON RESPONSIBLE

She loved her frog, knew that it could co-exist with Furl, and resolved never to ask it to do anything further. She also loved the adjuncts, who, once they listened to two or three sham reports from sham administrators, really did get on about the business of organizing themselves into a political union of sort, with ties to other such national organizations, and with even the possibility of striking, should the need arise.

She was torn out of the business of academic power politics by the buzzing of her cell phone, which she flipped open, and into which she said quietly:

"This is Nina Bannister."

A pause. She could hear the sound of breathing at the other end of the line.

"I said, this is Nina Bannister."

The husky rasp of a relatively deep female voice:

"I'm—I hate to bother you. I wasn't certain that I had the right to call."

"I'm sorry, who's…"

"This is Barbara Richardson."

It was Nina's turn to hesitate.

Probably because she knew nothing to say.

The woman at the other end, though, did have something to say:

"I wonder if we could possibly talk."

Nina surprised herself somewhat by answering:

"Yes, if you want."

Why should she talk to this woman, who had lied in public and helped to create the circumstances which now enfolded Rick like a moccasin?

Why?

But Nina did not understand her own motivations at times, and here she was saying:

"Where would you like to meet?"

"Could you come to my hotel? It's the Forest View, right downtown."

"Yes, I could do that."

"I'll have them send a car if you wish."

"No. I'm at the old gym. It's no more than half a mile from downtown and it's a pleasant enough afternoon. I can walk."

"All right. I'll see you soon then."

And Nina flipped the cell phone closed.

The Forest View was the city's oldest hotel, and in many ways the only establishment in a collection of Ramadas and Holidays that deserved to be described as in any way elegant. Its dark mahogany and mohair interior made one wince upon leaving the bright Mississippi mid-day, and Nina enjoyed the feeling of sinking into the carpet as she crossed to the reception desk.

The clerk smiled at her.

"Checking in, ma'am?"

"No, I'm expected. Richardson."

"Ah. That would be room 259."

"Thank you."

She ascended the stairs, turned right as the small sign instructed her to do, and in another minute was knocking at the door.

"It's open."

She pushed it and entered what was clearly a suite.

Tobacco smoke hung in the air, filtered gray and swirling in light that poured through a large picture window.

Barbara Richardson, from whose cigarette the smoke was emanating, turned from the window and faced her.

"Thank you for coming, Nina."

"It's all right."

The red brick buildings of the university lay spread behind and below the window. Barbara Richardson, dressed in a brick-colored business suit, seemed a part of the campus as she gestured toward the sofa.

"Please sit down."

"Thank you."

"I hope you don't object to the smoke."

"No. It's all right."

"I can call down if you'd like something to drink."

"I'm fine."

In a few seconds, the two women were seated, Nina on the sofa, Barbara Richardson on a brown leather chair. A glass-topped coffee table sat between them.

"I hardly know how to begin this. But when one thinks of it, there is just one way. I have to apologize and hope you will accept it."

Somehow words did not come for a second or so, and when they did, they seemed awkward.

Finally:

"Exactly what are you apologizing for?"

Although she knew very well.

But Barbara Richardson played gamely along.

"The account of yesterday's board meeting that I gave to the press last night was inaccurate."

"I know. I was at the meeting."

"Dr. Iverson—the provost—"

"I know who Dr. Iverson was."

"Of course. At any rate, he instructed me about what I was to say."

"And you went along."

"He's a very forceful man. At any rate, I felt it my responsibility to put the institution in the best light possible."

"Even if you had to lie to do so?"

"A university is in many senses merely a corporation. If you had been for many years in the corporate world, you would realize that in many instances appearances have to be maintained."

"I," Nina replied, "have been many years in the high school world. We try to maintain being honest. At least, that's what we tell our students to do."

A thin smile from across the table.

Then:

"Hopefully, none of your students will go on to—"

"Be you?"

"Lead a large corporation. Or a major university. If they do, they may find their illusions shattered."

"Well," said Nina, shaking her head, "I found mine pretty well shattered. So did Rick He's not a corporate guy either. He just gets paid to tell the truth. And the truth is, of course, that you let yourself be persuaded by a huge amount of money to go right along with Lucinda's ideas. Then, when you needed to back her up publically, you chickened out."

"Yes. I suppose that's as good a way as any to put it."

"That's the only way to put it, Ms. Richardson."

She could have said *Barbara*, but she didn't want to.

Nor, she realized, did she care much to be called *Nina* again.

Barbara Richardson stubbed her cigarette out on an ashtray which sat in the precise center of the coffee table. She turned slightly, so that she was looking out of the window and over the university. She either saw or failed to see something, Nina was not sure which. She either followed it for a time or gave up looking for it, then turned back and said, quietly:

"We end so far from where we started. One border crossed. One step taken. Against our better judgment. After a time we forget who we were, who we ever wanted to be."

Nina did not speak, happy, she realized, because those things had not happened to her.

Nor would they have happened last night.

She had no regrets about who she was, or had ever been.

Because they were the same thing.

And they would have been, even if the couch in Rick's house had been bare.

This was not the case for Barbara Richardson, though, who now was looking at her, very intently.

"I have to ask you something. And it's very important to me that you answer as carefully as possible."

"All right."

"Is it possible—even remotely possible—that Richard Barnes could have killed Dr. Iverson?"

"No."

"You don't know where he was for those two hours."

"That's true."

"The story was on his computer. As I understand it, a detailed story."

"I know."

"He and Dr. Iverson were fiercely antagonistic."

"I know."

The woman across from her looked at her watch, then seemed to sigh.

"I'm sorry. I must catch a flight back to Vicksburg in little more than an hour."

She rose, as did Nina.

"Thank you for coming. It meant a lot to me. I needed to apologize, though I'm not certain it does much good. It certainly has not helped Mr. Barnes."

The two began walking toward the door.

"Rick will be all right."

"I hope so. I sincerely do."

"He didn't do this thing."

Barbara Richardson opened the door, and Nina went through it, out into the hallway.

"I had my doubts. The way all signs seem to point. Despite your trust in Mr. Barnes, there is a part of me that wishes him to be guilty."

"What?"

"I said there is a part of me that wishes him to be guilty."

"Why for heaven's sakes?"

"Because," said Barbara Richardson, "if he's not the murderer, then I know who is."

"Who?"

"I am responsible for the whole thing," she said, and shut the door.

A few minutes later, Nina was in the middle of downtown, standing on a sidewalk, talking on her cell phone with Jackson Bennett.

"Jackson, I've just heard something very strange."

A pause.

She could hear his heavy breathing.

"I have too, Nina. I was about to call you."

"What did you hear, Jackson?"

"I don't want to talk about it on the phone. We need to meet."

"All right. My bungalow?"

"No, too many people know you live there. I want it to be private."

She thought about that one for a time and finally said:

"There's the old bell tower. I think it's open to the public. Let's meet up there, maybe in fifteen minutes or so."

"Done."

And she snapped the two halves of the phone together.

The bell tower was a huge obelisk located in the exact center of town, and one was forced to negotiate more than a hundred steps to reach the top. Nina climbed slowly, holding the dark metal handrail and trying not to get dizzy as she circled, paused, breathed hard for a bit, circled, paused...and, through the thick, semi-circular openings in the wall that could have served as gun-ports in a fortress, watched the middle of the trees, then the tops of the trees, then the nearer buildings of campus, then the outlying buildings of the campus, then the city, then beyond the city...and then the autumn sky, now completely blue except for a few wispy clouds.

Finally, she was there, the bell hanging before her like a great ugly brass evening gown with no glitter, and the somber, dark-stained copper look of a thousand dead pennies.

Wooden benches lined the walls on each side of the tower, which, at night was illuminated by dimly-glowing bulbs attached to fixtures just below the roof line near each corner. About two feet above each bench, and precisely in the center of the wall, were the windows, looking out on the campus.

She walked around the bell, leaned her elbows on unyielding dark red granite...the walls were a foot and a half thick—and peered through.

Golden and blue on campus, rainbowed beyond, where the town still glowed and midwayed, its fast food restaurants, car lots, intersections, freeways, and river bridges twinkling, flashing and radiating one garish color after another, with red red! *red*! clearly predominant.

Five minutes later, Jackson Bennett arrived, and a minute after that they were seated on one of the benches.

He took a deep breath, paused, and finally said:

"This may be difficult for you to hear, Nina. But I wanted you to get it from me first hand."

There was something about Jackson's demeanor that made her delay her own account of the conversation with Barbara Richardson.

"Go ahead, Jackson."

"This concerns Rick's article about the provost."

"You mean the one that was found on his word processor?"

"That's the one."

"Rick didn't write it."

"Are you sure about that, Nina?"

"Of course I am. He wasn't at his house when the article was written. And anyway, what is there about the article that's so special?"

"Because it's accurate."

"It's what?"

"Accurate. One hundred per cent. Every number."

"Are you telling me that the provost was actually…"

"Embezzling money. Millions of dollars, out of the faculty retirement fund. He's been running the scam for years, apparently."

"That's incredible."

"Yes, but it's true. And talk about some shame-faced administrators. A day or so ago, they were told they were useless, and they were fired. Then they think they might be re-hired. And then a bunch of them—the comptroller, the Director of Financial Management, and on and on and on—realize this one guy could have been siphoning off huge sums of money right under their noses and storing it in a secret bank account in the Azores."

She thought about it for a while, then shook her head.

"Jackson the fact remains. Rick didn't write it. He was walking in the town when the article was written."

"I know, that's his story."

"That's the truth. Rick wouldn't lie."

Bennett arose, walked in a tight circle, then looked at her and asked:

"Nina, who the hell *else* could have written it? From what Adam Marsh told me half an hour or so ago, it's a supreme job of getting at the truth. There are facts in here that nobody but an ace investigative reporter could possibly have come up with."

"But somebody else did, Jackson."

"Okay. So somebody else did. That somebody needs to step forward, and now. Because the truth of the story makes things look even worse for Rick, I'm sure you see that. First, only a great reporter—like Rick—could have written it. Second, it would have given the provost every reason to come to Rick's house and threaten him."

"Yes, I see that."

"And there is tougher problem."

"Just what we need. All right, what is this *tougher* problem?"

"*The Gazette* is going with this story; they have to."

"I see that."

"The problem is, whom do they attribute it to?"

"What do you mean?"

"Nina, this story may have saved the retirement benefits of thousands of professors. The account is identified. This money can be confiscated now and returned to the fund it was taken from. If Rick wrote this story, it could mean a Pulitzer for him."

"And life imprisonment."

"Well, there's that."

"Has anybody talked to Rick about this?"

"March had just come from the jail when he called me. Rick still swears he didn't write it."

"Then he didn't. And I'm sure he won't want credit."

"But listen, if he…"

They were interrupted by the buzzing of Jackson's cell phone.

"I better take this, Nina."

"Sure, go ahead."

She rose and walked to the other side of the tower, gazing down on the campus while Jackson's low soft voice, indistinct now, rumbled behind her.

Scenes unfolded in her mind. They were all unworldly, bizarre, moving everywhere and nowhere, and having neither beginning nor end.

She found herself thinking about what Barbara Richardson had told her.

How could she have killed the provost?

How? The two had been seen together after the Jumbotron show. She had seen the provost receive his provocative message, then stride off toward Rick's.

Could she have beaten him there?

And written the piece that was found on the word processor?

And why was she asking Nina if Rick was guilty?

If she herself had committed the crime, then she clearly knew that Rick was not guilty.

Behind her Jackson Bennett stood up.

"Something else has come up, Nina."

"What?"

"It's Barbara Richardson."

"That's what I came to tell you."

Jackson cocked his head:

"What? What are you talking about?"

"Barbara Richardson. Has she confessed to killing the provost?"

"No, she's dead. Murdered no more than ten minutes ago in her hotel room. Somebody stuck a butcher knife in her heart."

CHAPTER TWENTY THREE: THE WOMAN FROM VICKSBURG

The two of them simply sat where they were for a time, staring at each other.

The movie, stranger and stranger, continued to flow past, mingling with the clouds.

Finally Jackson spoke:

"Why did you think she confessed?"

"Because she did confess."

"When?"

"Twenty minutes ago."

"Where?"

"In her hotel room."

"To whom?"

"To me."

"You were in her hotel room?"

"Yes."

"My God. What did she say?"

"She asked me if I were certain that Rick had not killed the provost. I told her I was absolutely certain. We were standing in the doorway. She said that if Rick didn't kill him, then she knew who did. I asked her who it was, and she answered, 'I am.' Then she shut the door."

But that doesn't make sense. Why would Barbara Richardson have wanted to kill Charles Iverson?"

"I don't know. I do know that she was with him when he got the message that Rick had ostensibly written to him. He read the message, then, according to witnesses, took off to Rick's house as fast as he could.

How could she have beaten him there, gotten in, found the shotgun, and murdered him?"

Robinson shook his head:

"No, it doesn't make sense. But that's the least of our worries now."

"What's the most of our worries now?"

"The most of our worries now, is what the hell we're going to do with you."

"What do you mean?"

"I mean, you were clearly the last person to see her alive, other than the killer. And she confessed to you that she murdered the provost. It may have been impossible for her to have done it, and she may have had no motive for it—but like it or not, she did confess."

"I still don't..."

And then she understood.

"I have to tell the police these things, don't I?"

"I think you do, Nina."

"And they're going to think I did it."

"I don't know what they're going to think."

"I've already been arrested for murder once."

"I know. But they've got to understand that you have no motive for wanting to kill Barbara Richardson."

"I didn't have a motive for wanting to kill Charles Iverson. It doesn't seem to matter to the police in this town. They look at Nina Bannister and think Charles Manson."

"Nina, for now, I want you to disappear. Ultimately, you'll have to make a statement to the police, and, as an officer of the court as well as your attorney, I'm obligated to produce you. But that doesn't mean I have to do it just this instant. Let me go downtown and at least gather as many facts about this thing as possible. You wander on campus. Find some building and go inside. Keep out of everybody's way. In an hour or so, after I know what's really happened and how, I'll call you. Then we'll plot our strategy."

"All right, Jackson."

And with that, they descended the tower.

She said good-bye to Jackson Bennett and then wandered.

There was a small park in the center of the downtown area. She entered it, spotted a bench, and sat down.

It was now late afternoon, and shadows were lengthening. The light was turning golden.

A few children were throwing Frisbees.

What to do?

She thought.

And then it came to her.

There was, of course, only one thing to do.

She rose from the bench, turned, and walked back toward the campus.

Within ten minutes, she was entering the library.

She was relieved to find it open, and she was equally relieved to find it as deserted as it had been when she'd first visited it with Old Whittington of Classics.

A haunted house.

The thoughts and dreams of all man and womankind, slumbering peacefully within these musty volumes.

Sophocles.

Homer.

Virgil.

Horace.

And then another aisle, and yet another aisle, the centuries slipping past.

Chaucer.

Shakespeare.

Milton.

And another aisle and another aisle...

… and then she was home.

"Hello, Jane," she whispered.

There it was.

Emma.

She touched the cover and seemed to breathe in the lines that had always been there for her.

"A mind lively and at ease can do with seeing nothing. And can see nothing that does not answer."

Your mind has been lively, Nina. Very lively with all the revolutionary events going on around it, inundating it.

But it can no longer afford to be at ease.

Think, Nina. Force yourself to think.

There are enough elements in the puzzle now.

Something doesn't fit.

Find that something.

Rick's life may depend on it.

Your own life may depend on it.

Go over what has happened. Your first meeting with Lucinda; first meeting—an unpleasant enough one, heaven knows, with the provost; his breaking it off because he had to fly out to attend a convention of college and university administrators; meeting the adjuncts at Nick's; coming here, to this library, with old Whittington; then the unforgettable faculty meeting the following morning; the board meeting where she was to see for the first time Barbara Richardson; the next adjunct meeting; the meeting with Lucinda in her office; the—

—but no, something had happened before that.

The encounter with—what was his name? Mathieson?

He'd learned about it while mowing the lawn. Learned that his career was over.

Then the encounter with two outraged women, one of them the provost's wife.

Then the—

No, go back.

Lively and at ease, lively and at ease...

What had Mathieson said?

"I should not even have been here today. I was supposed to be at a convention of college and university administrators.

In Hattiesburg.

Hattiesburg.

Events had come up, making it impossible for him to attend.

Hattiesburg.

But go on, Nina. Let it all flow past.

The cabin with Rick; the meeting at the stadium; the fight; the announcement; the—

—back. Back...

The provost talking to that ring of reporters.

"I only learned about these shocking events some hours ago. I flew directly back here from Vicksburg, where I had been attending a convention."

Vicksburg.

Hattiesburg.

But that would mean...

Where else had she heard *Vicksburg*?

And there were other places.

The Azores.

He had been funneling money into a secret account.

In the Azores.

Think, Nina, think.

Her mind was not at ease now.

And into it came Rick's description of his early days with the provost.

'We got along fine the first few months he was here. He and his wife even invited me over for dinner. I reciprocated.'

I reciprocated.

Vicksburg.

Not Hattiesburg.

The Azores.

I reciprocated.

"But who," she whispered to herself, "was also in..."

Then she remembered.

"My God."

Barbara Richardson.

"Crossing lines. Going too far. And then—we're not the people we once were."

Barbara Richardson.

"Because I was responsible for his death."

"And you really did kill him," Nina whispered. "You really did."

She stood for a while, simply trying to grasp what had happened.

Then she whispered again, at the book which lay beneath her palm:

"Thank you again, dear Jane. You're always there for me. Thank you again."

Then she left the library.

Then she called Jackson.

One hour later he and she—both having insisted on being present—were in the second of two police cars that pulled up to a stately Victorian mansion on the west side of campus.

Several uniformed officers approached the door and rang the bell.

By the time the door opened there was a ring of people surrounding it.

Amy Iverson, professionally dressed in a blue business suit which contrasted starkly with her flaming red hair, scanned the circle.

Her eyes came to rest on Nina.

"I'm sorry," she said. "I was coming down to turn myself in. You may not believe that, of course. I wouldn't if I were in your place. I would never have let Rick be convicted, either. It's just that I needed time. I had to do them both. They both deserved it. It would have been best to do them at the same time. But I never had that chance. After I shot Charles last night, I needed time to do the woman. I don't want to say her name. She doesn't deserve even to have a name. But at any rate, someone had to take the blame until I had time to do, today, just now, what was necessary. I don't know why she let me in. It was as though she knew what she deserved, almost welcomed it. I do, too. I welcome it. And so this ends it. Let's go."

So saying, she walked out toward the first squad car in the row of cars.

CHAPTER TWENTY FOUR: EXPLANATIONS

A lamp was burning on the central table in Rick Barnes' back yard, and the four of them—she, Rick, Adam Marsh, and Peter Stockton—cast their shadows in dim light.

It was ten p.m.

Sounds of the campus could be heard buzzing and wailing in the distance.

The air hung redolent of summer spent and fruit ready to begin fall decay.

Four cans of beer stood on the table, each being taken up, drained, and put back, one after another.

Rick, who'd been released two hours earlier in the evening, leaned forward.

"Do you think, Adam, that she would really have turned herself in?"

Adam Marsh merely shrugged:

"No idea. If she could do the things she did—who knows how such a person's mind works? At any rate, because of Nina here, it's all a moot point."

Rick:

"What can I say, Nina. I owe you my life."

She took a sip of beer and shook her head:

"I'm not sure that's true. She was so enraged, so embittered. She wasn't trying to get away with anything. Or rather, not ultimately. The first murder was brilliantly contrived to make you seem guilty. But that was only to buy time for her to commit the second one. After that, her job was done. She was probably even proud of what she'd done."

Jackson Bennett:

"How did you figure it all out, Nina?"

She put the can carefully on the table.

"Vicksburg isn't Hattiesburg."

"Pardon?"

"When I first visited the office of the provost, Iverson cut the meeting short because he had to fly to a conference of college and university administrators. As well as I can remember, he didn't say where the conference was. But Matheson, did say."

Barnes nodded:

"I remember. We found him in his office when we were in the administration building, on our way to see Lucinda."

"That's right. He said he'd been scheduled to attend that conference too. In Hattiesburg. But something had come up and caused him to postpone the trip. The problem is, that evening, just before you had the fight, Iverson told a reporter, almost in passing, that his flight had just gotten in from Vicksburg. It didn't make sense. So I started thinking: when had the name Vicksburg come up? The answer was, of course, during the board meeting. Barbara Richardson introduced herself as CEO of Adorn Cosmetics..."

Both men at the table said, simultaneously:

"Based in Vicksburg."

"Yes. So there was that. And there was also Barbara Richardson's tan."

"Pardon?"

"That day after the board had met, and she came to tell Peter Stockton and the two of us, Rick, that the board was going along with Lucinda's plans. Lucinda talked about what a good tan she had, and she said, not needing to lug a husband around, she'd just come back from some days in the Azores. That just lay dormant in the back of my mind—my mind being lively and at ease—until earlier this afternoon, Jackson, when you told me about Iverson's embezzlement scheme."

"He was," Rick said, nodding, "funneling money to an account in the Azores."

"The two of them," Marsh chimed in, "were planning to leave the country together and live like millionaires in the Azores."

Rick:

"But wouldn't people have suspected?"

Marsh shook his head:

"The money was too expertly hidden. And as for Iverson? He leaves the country and lives in an island paradise. Who's to blame him for that? He had no idea his wife was onto this. Clearly their marriage hadn't been much for the last few years. He probably thought she'd accept generous divorce terms and never miss him."

Nina:

"Of course, what he didn't realize was that she'd known about the affair for years. She's got a vicious temper, Rick, you and I saw that. But she didn't lose that temper. She kept it under control and planned a slow and cruel revenge."

Adam Marsh:

"It's out now; I heard early this evening from some of the interrogating officers. She hired a private investigator, I believe out of New Orleans, to shadow her husband. He was at first supposed to just dig up dirt on the romantic angle. But he was good, and found out about the embezzlement as well. So Amy knew everything."

Nina continued:

"That was how Amy could write the letter that was delivered to Iverson at the stadium. While he was reading it, she was here at your place, Rick, composing the document the police found on your word processor."

"But how did she know about my..."

"...your house? You told me that yourself, Rick. You said, when the provost and his wife first came to the campus, they invited you to dinner. And you reciprocated."

"That's right. I remember the evening they came over."

"And you probably told them how you loved your little neighborhood. And how safe it was."

"And how," he said, quietly, "I never lock the front door."

"She also would have had the chance to see your shotgun, hanging there like a trophy, just as it was until last night."

"When she used it to blow away her husband..."

"...just as though he were an animal."

They were silent for a time.

Finally, Nina asked:

"Adam, what have you heard about Lucinda?"

The attorney pursed his lips.

"It's not the best situation."

"No, I didn't think it would be."

"She's going to be taking a leave of absence."

"That's what they're calling it?"

"They're telling her it's a kind of vacation. Actually, she'll be undergoing psychological evaluation at an..."

"Institute."

"Yes. For want of a better term."

"And she agreed to this?"

"Yes. As far as she's concerned, she's resuming duties of the presidency in a month or so. If she had refused, the university's attorneys had collected enough information—mainly Whittington's testimony—to have her removed for cause."

A pause.

Then:

"The university community doesn't know the full extent of the problem. They've been told though, that President Herndon will be leaving the residence tomorrow at 11 a.m. There will be a gala brunch. Lucinda will address the crowd. A last flourish, so to speak. We're invited, of course."

Silence for a time.

Rick:

"And so, Nina."

"Yes."

"The job you've been offered?"

She shook her head.

"I don't know, Rick. With Lucinda leaving…"

"I understand."

"I feel so empty. So much has happened."

"Sure."

"All I can think to do now is go back to the little Hobbit House and get some sleep. Maybe tomorrow the world—well, it won't be the same. You. Lucinda. No, it won't be the same. But maybe after some sleep, it will make more sense."

She honestly believed this.

And she was completely wrong.

CHAPTER TWENTY FIVE: FAREWELL, FAREWELL, LUCINDA

Nina pulled her pants up and buttoned them. She was mulling over what was in front of her. Lucy Herndon with a diagnosis of Alzheimer's disease. Unthinkable. Impossible. Unbelievable. She pulled on her orange blouse with the bow ties and buttoned it up. Looking up at herself in the mirror, she pulled up the ties and tied a loose bow. She sighed. She sat on the bed and pulled on her shoes and socks. What could she possibly say to her? Shaking her head, she pushed open the door and walked toward campus.

Nina entered the president's mansion through the side door she'd used before. Today, the room seemed gray, as if shades were closed during a cloudy day. The chairs were gray, the coffee table was gray, and Lucinda, standing motionless on the other side of the room, seemed gray. For a moment, it was silent in the room

"Oh, Lucy!" cried Nina, crossing the room quickly and grabbing Lucy in a big bear hug.

Lucy was crying. Her shoulders shook gently as she bent her head onto Nina's shoulder.

They stood together, arms wrapped around each other, rocking slowly back and forth.

"I can't believe it!" said Nina.

"I know, I know, Nina, I'm so, so, sorry for what I did. I would never knowingly hurt you. You know that, don't you?" Lucy pulled her head back and looked searchingly into Nina's eyes.

Nina dropped her arms and began to pat Lucy gently on her upper arm. "Shhhh, I know, I know, it's okay. It's forgotten. Today is about you. What are you going to do, Lucy?"

Lucy pulled Nina over to the couch and they sat side by side, turned so they faced each other.

"It's all so overwhelming, Nina. Living alone, I didn't realize that I was "sun-downing" in the evenings. I would watch a little television and go to bed. I'm still in the early stages, so if I had an evening meeting, it would stimulate me enough to be aware and remember, but at home, apparently, I would just disappear into thoughts. No one knows how long I've been this way, but, since I live alone, I could have had symptoms for years that no one knew, but now it's harder and harder to hold myself together."

"I'm afraid they will ask you to step down, Lucy. What will you do? Is there medicine that can help you? What can I do?"

"They've started me on Aricept, but it's hard to believe that little pill can make any difference. I have a phone number and an email address for a person from the Alzheimer's Association at the hospital. I suppose I should start there with my questions. It's so hard to plan what to expect, although I think we both know…" Her voice trailed off.

"I wish we could live closer, Lucy. I've decided to go back to Bay St. Lucy. I don't suppose you could relocate down there?"

"No, no. This is what I know. I'm afraid that a new city would confuse me more. I'm afraid that losing my job will confuse me more. I'm afraid!" She clutched Nina's hand. "Thank goodness for Professor Whittington. He's a dear, dear, old friend. Do you know him?"

Nina blinked. "Yes, I met him two days ago."

"He and Thomas and I were all so fond of each other. He has a guest room in the home he has across the street from campus. He's making arrangements for me to stay there, and has offered to find a companion to stay with me when he has to leave. Although I don't think I need a companion right now."

"That's a great idea, Lucy! You could still go to the library, maybe continue the research on projects you haven't had time for with your busy job as president."

Lucy nodded her head absent-mindedly.

"Oh! What are you doing here? I need to go and make my grand entrance as I do each time I meet with the faculty. I'm sorry, dear, I'm going to have to ask you to leave." She stood up and gestured to the side door. "I don't know who you are, but if you'll just go now, I can see if my secretary can arrange a meeting this afternoon in my office." She smiled.

Stunned at this sudden appearance of the dementia, Nina stood up and moved toward the door. She turned. "Lucy?"

"Yes?"

"I will always love you."

"Thank you, dear."

And Nina left the building, closing the door gently behind her.

It was a luscious early September morning, wisps of clouds hanging motionless in the mid-September central Mississippi sky, and the scents of bougainvillea's and late flowering marigolds inebriating the senses of those present

There were not so many of them, given the occasion. No major public announcement had been made. A few close friends, some scattered administrators and faculty members. It was not, except possibly in the mind of

Lucinda Herndon herself, a particularly joyous occasion.

The press had been asked not to come, and, out of deference to the Grande Dame of Ellerton University, had stayed away.

Nina was there, of course, standing with Peter Stockton, Jackson, Rick, and Adam Marsh in the front yard of the residence. There were perhaps fifteen others, all watching Whittington of Classics as, eyes moist, he bent and croaked like the old man he was into a standing microphone.

"It is the end of an era," he was saying. "How well I remember their coming. Thomas and Lucinda, the world in front of them, and this grand university, the center of that world. All of us young Turks of the faculty thought they could do no wrong. The life we created here, in those dazzling days when it always seemed to be summer or, at worst, the first cool time of the fall, when the colors became so magnificent. That was the life of the mind. Achilles strode these paths, and Oedipus in despair wandered over them. There were publications, of course, for we all loved to write. Not because our careers hinged upon it, but because of some innate drive that made us do so. You could not have stopped our writing any more than you could have stopped our gatherings, on each other's yards, in any number of the scattered watering holes. We were the Algonquin Round Table and Lucinda was our Dorothy Parker, or at other times I fancied myself a budding Tolkien, carrying Middle Earth in my mind and discoursing mightily to C. S. Lewis, albeit of some other name."

He stopped for a time to take out a handkerchief.

Peter Stockton used the pause to lean over Nina and whisper:

"I'm going to miss her. It won't be the same."

Nina, looking up into the craggy face:

"Your donation? The buildings?"

He shook his head.

"Not now. It's going to be the same way it was. And I don't want to support it anymore."

Rick Barnes' voice seeped through their group:

"Look, on the front porch. It's Lucinda."

And she had, in fact, had appeared behind the great glass doors, awaiting Whittington's introduction.

She was wearing the same dark blue outfit she'd worn when Nina had breakfast with her a thousand years before.

"She always likes to make an entrance," Nina whispered, so low that she was probably the only one who heard. "That's what she told me on the morning we went and she addressed the faculty. She always likes to throw open those doors, with great dramatic flair, and stride out into the campus."

Someone apparently had heard, for Adam Barnes responded:

"She'll be doing it this time for the last time."

None of them spoke.

Whittington:

"And now it is time."

He took a sprig of some herb from his pocket, and ground it between his fingers, letting the crushed particles fall on the moist and glistening grass.

"Rosemary, as the dear Ophelia would have said, is for memory."

Complete silence.

Then he turned and faced the doorway, saying:

"Come to us, fair Ophelia. And bid us, this one last time, adieu."

Nina could remember seeing Lucinda Herndon's wide, dazzling smile, reflected in a sunburst on the sparkling glass door.

She remembered the grand, sweeping arm gesture as the president threw open the doors.

It was then that the bomb, which tests later showed had been wired to the door, exploded.

Even some days later, Nina could recall the massive blow, like being kicked by a horse against a wall, the thrust spread evenly over her entire body, one thrust crushing her chest and the other snapping her neck and the base of her skull. She could remember thinking that someone had opened an oven door too quickly, the heat all rushing out and up into her face, burning her.

Then she was unconscious for a time.

When she awoke, there were the sirens, and people reaching down to her. And of course there were screams everywhere.

"Nina! Nina!"

She had no idea where the cries were coming from, or who might have been calling for her.

She also did not know how she got to her feet. Looking back, she decided that she must have been, at least at some point, crawling. But—this much she knew—she was on her feet when the stretcher carrying Lucinda Herndon was carried by beneath her.

She wondered where all the blood was coming from. It covered the stretcher, the sheets..."

Then Rick Barnes was there. He had somehow appeared, and was standing close by Nina, his arm around her.

Lucinda Herndon was looking up at both of them, but only seeing Rick, at whom she smiled:

"You've come for me, Thomas!"

And then she died.

CHAPTER TWENTY SIX: TWO CONVERSATIONS WITH PEOPLE NOT PRESENT

The letter read as follows:

"I'm here now at the base of the stone jetty. It's a good place, where I do a lot of crabbing. The town is deserted now, pretty much. School has begun, and the tourists are gone.

I've just come from feeding Furl. It's as though I was never away.

Out in the ocean, right now, as I'm writing this, I can see my two porpoises, leaping out of the water, one after another, maybe half a mile out, where the water is green in the afternoon sun.

Leaping, leaping…

Now they're gone.

I think about you a lot of course, and have, ever since I've been back home. I'm so happy you weren't hurt in the blast. Of course, no one was, except for Lucy. We were all standing too far back. And maybe it's for the best this way. She would have had to live a long time, with her mind ebbing away a little more every day.

I've been told that they're still trying to find some kind of clue that might tell them who set the bomb, but I don't think they ever will; Lucy had just made too many enemies. One of them— maybe several of them—was responsible for it.

But, like I say, I've got a feeling they'll never find out who.

Yes, maybe it's for the best, this way.

I won't forget you, Rick, or the time with you. The first night, when you came and interviewed me. And that remarkable day, when impossible things kept happening."

Your house. Your cabin.

Just how easy it all felt.

But...

...but I think I'll stay home now. This is my home. My life is here. As for the job Lucy offered me—well, it might have been exciting if she had truly won, and if her revolution had truly taken place. But she didn't win. And revolutions—real ones—maybe only happen in books.

At any rate, Ellerton's semester has begun now, and the same old story is going on.

Bureaucrats with big salaries and nothing to do.

Researchers pouring out tons of things no one can understand.

The same old story.

I hope you understand.

Thank you for everything, Rick."

The letter was signed:
"Nina."

After she'd written it, she folded it carefully and slipped it into the stamped, blue envelope that had already been addressed.

Then she took it to her Vespa, which had been chained not far from the base of the jetty.

There was a post box several hundred yards to the south on Breakers Boulevard, where she mailed the letter.

Then she drove back home.

The sun was going down. Its glow capped the waves golden.

She was walking now, her canvas slippers wet with the seawater that she allowed to splash upon them.

Hello.

Hello to you.

I haven't talked to you in some time.

Don't worry about it. I'm always here. You know that.

I'm sorry. I'm so sorry. I…

Don't.

It's just that…it seemed right with him somehow. Like it was with us.

That's good, Nina. You're alive. That's what happens to people sometime. Living people, like you.

But it wouldn't have been like us.

No, of course not. Nothing could ever be like that.

And still…I'm so sorry. So sorry.

Don't worry. It's like the song. You know? The one we loved so much?

The Sisters of Mercy?

Yes. That song. We aren't lovers like that and, besides, it would still be all right.

And is it all right?

Of course, it's all right. It will always be all right between us. Forever.

Thank you.

I love you, Nina.

I love you too, Frank.

And she went home.

EPILOGUE

Mind Change is just a fantasy.

It would have to be, would it not?

It could not be true.

Surely, American universities do not pay millions of dollars to administrators with titles such as Associate Vice President for Curriculum Control.

Surely, the research done at major state universities is always directly relevant to the lives of students at these institutions. Surely, full time faculty never teach as few as three or four courses per year and never go to needless conferences in various cities around the world, where all of their expenses are paid.

Surely, most of the students in American universities are not taught by adjunct faculty, who are paid approximately two thousand dollars per course.

Surely, there is no such university president as Lucinda Herndon, and never could be.

Surely, this is all just a fantasy.

It would have to be.

Wouldn't it?

THE END

ABOUT THE AUTHORS

 Pam Britton (T'Gracie) Reese is an Assistant Professor in the Communication Science and Disorders Department at Indiana/Purdue University at Fort Wayne. Previously, she worked as a speech pathologist in schools in private practice. She was also a supervisor in communication disorders at Ohio University. She likes nothing better, professionally, than helping small, silent two-year-old boys start talking. She has also published books about autism with LinguiSystems for the last 15 years. *The Circle of Autism* was previously published online at *ken*again e-magazine*.

Joe Reese is a novelist, playwright, storyteller, and college teacher. He has published four novels, several plays, and a number of stories and articles. When he's not teaching (English and German), he enjoys visiting elementary schools, where he tells stories from his Katie Dee novels and talks to students about writing. He and his wife Pam have three children: Kate, Matthew, and Sam.

OTHER BOOKS BY T'GRACIE AND JOE REESE:

Sea Change
Set Change
Game Change
Oil Change
Frame Change
Sex Change
Climate Change

www.ingramcontent.com/pod-product-compliance
Lightning Source LLC
Chambersburg PA
CBHW050401260626
47156CB00003B/828